The
Bakers

The
Bakers

William Carter Burnham

ReadersMagnet, LLC

C O N T E N T S

CHAPTER 1 1
CHAPTER 2 5
CHAPTER 3 11
CHAPTER 4 17
CHAPTER 5 22
CHAPTER 6 29
CHAPTER 7 33
CHAPTER 8 39
CHAPTER 9 47
CHAPTER 10 52
CHAPTER 11 58
CHAPTER 12 63
CHAPTER 13 68
CHAPTER 14 73
CHAPTER 15 77
CHAPTER 16 85
CHAPTER 17 91
CHAPTER 18 95
CHAPTER 19 103
CHAPTER 20 111
CHAPTER 21 117
CHAPTER 22 122
CHAPTER 23 129

CHAPTER 1

Noah Martin went to Texas in 1840. He has lived there for the last ten years. Now he is back in Alabama, trying to convince Bud Baker, his brother-in-law, to sell his farm and go back to Texas with him. That night after supper, they were sitting on the back of a wagon, with a pint of corn liquor between them.

Noah picked up the bottle of whiskey, turned it up, and took a swig, then made a sour face.

He exhaled, "That is some good drinkin' there boy."

"Made it myself," said Bud.

"I'm tellin' ya Bud, if you see this country, you will fall in love with it. Texas ain't like nothin' you ever seen before."

Bud looked out over the yard. "Noah, it ain't been that long since we was fightin' injuns here. I done got too old for all that."

"They are out there. I won't lie to ya about that, but they don't mess around much in East Texas anymore. Bud, a fellow I know left his 50-acre farm in Ohio. Now he works at his 300-acre cotton farm in Texas. The thing is, he clears about 5 new acres every year. Now you just think about that."

Bud took the bottle from Noah. "Yep, all that shore sounds good alright, but leavin' here is asking a lot of my family."

"It would be a bright future for them kids," said Noah.

The two men talked on into the night. Noah was pretty convincing. He knew his brother-in-law. He has heard him say many times about buying more land, and raising more cotton. About growing his herd of cattle.

Bud's wife yelled through the screen door. "Getting late boys, about bedtime."

Bud lay awake thinking about his conversation with Noah. The idea of owning so much land.

That was every farmer's dream. Just think, 1000-acre farm, maybe bigger. Cotton, corn cattle. He had a restless night's sleep. His mind raced, thinking about this idea of Noah's. A foolish thing to even consider but what if he could go there and build a big farm, big enough to support his kids and their kids. My word, what a dream!

Mary opened the bedroom door. "Well Mr. Bud, are you goin' to sleep all day?" Bud swung his feet off the bed. "Damn you Noah. Come and turn my head inside out."

They didn't talk about Texas all day, but that night as the family sat at the supper table. Bud said grace, then they began to eat their supper. He and his wife, Mary Jane, had four children, Jennie age seventeen, Rob fifteen, Patty twelve, and Ted nine. Without looking up, Bud asks the question. "How do y'all feel about pullin' up stakes and goin' to Texas?" They all stopped eating, and looked at each other.

"Are you sayin' you want to leave here?" asked Mary.

"I am saying it is something we need to think about. It could be a good move for us, especially you kids. It could be a good future for all of you."

"What's in Texas that we ain't got here?" Jennie asked.

"Land," said Noah, "miles and miles of open space, like you never seen. Good land, rich farmland."

"I don't know what to say," said Mary.

"Don't say nothin'," said Bud, "I want all of you to think on it. We will talk more later."

That night after supper, Jennie and Patty helped their mother clean up the kitchen. Then Jennie took her brothers and sister outside.

"Well, what do you think about going to Texas?" she asked. Rob spoke up, "I kinda like the idea."

"I don't know," said Patty.

"Uncle Noah shore is taken with it." Said Rob.

The next day was spent talking about moving to Texas, as they did their daily chores.

At supper, the Baker family was sitting around the table, they all knew Bud would ask the question.

"Jennie, I know you kids have talked, so let's hear it."

"Well paw," Jennie paused, "to make it short, whatever you decide is fine with us. As for me, if we are all together that's all that counts."

Bud looked around the table, "I want you kids to know it ain't going be no easy thing, leavin' here, travelin' all the way to Texas. Starting a new life. Building up a new farm from scratch. Shore ain't gone be easy."

Bud looked at his wife, "Well Mary, how 'bout you? What you got to say?"

"Recon I will be fine, as long as I am with my family. I ain't crazy about it."

Her mother was insecure and always unsure of herself, and afraid to make a decision. Bud watched his wife slowly allow Jennie to take over the duties of the house. Her brothers and sister came to Jennie with their problems, and for advice. She was a truly remarkable young lady.

It took Bud three months to sell his farm and buy a wagon and horses that could make the trip. Bud had six beef cows, five cows and a bull. He planned to take them with him.

"Plenty of good grass," Noah told him, "want be no trouble raisin' some cows."

"I will take them two milk cows too," said Bud.

CHAPTER 2

It was late winter, Noah suggested they wait till spring to get started. When April came they were all packed and ready to go. Each of them had their own memories they would be leaving behind.

Noah could see the reluctance in their faces as they loaded up and were about to head out, "Look ahead, won't do no good lookin' back," said Noah.

They took a less traveled road through Alabama, Mississippi and Louisiana. They crossed the red river and now they were in Texas at last. It was late afternoon when they caught up with another family that was camped just off the road. Noah held up his hand, for them to stop the wagon. Bud joined him.

"What's wrong, why we stopping?"

"Somebody camped up ahead there."

"What's wrong with that?"

"Mighty unusual, folks stopping this time of day."

"Ah, maybe they got trouble," said Bud.

"Maybe, you stay here."

Noah rode toward the camp. The wagon was sitting just off the road under a big tree. He unlatched his pistol, so it would be easier to get to. When he was about twenty yards from the camp, he stopped. He saw children coming from the trees. Then he saw somebody he knew.

"Damn, I know him," thought Noah, "that's Albert Nelson."

He took off his hat and held it up over his head. Albert saw Noah waving his hat in the air. "By golly, that is Noah." Can't be two of them in this part of the world. He motioned for Noah to come in.

The two men met about three years ago. They were both working for a cotton farmer and became good friends. Their paths crossed again about eight months ago. They talked about going back east and bringing their families here to Texas. They both left Texas about the same time. Albert went to Tennessee for his wife and kids.

"Well, well, what the hell you doin' in these parts?" Albert asked.

"Same as you I recon. Got my family with me."

Albert told him why they were camped there. His wife, June, took ill and died. They buried her yesterday.

"I shore am sorry to hear that."

"I never figured on this," said Albert. "She ain't never been sick before."

Albert lowered his head and with a trembling voice, "She was a good woman." They didn't speak for a few minutes.

"What ya gonna do now?" asked Noah.

"That's a good question. Getting' them kids to move on and leave their mama is gonna be hard. Be hard for me."

Noah and Bud decided to make camp close to the Nelsons. Jennie and her mother cooked supper and invited the Nelsons to join them. Noah and Albert sat and talked half the night.

The next morning, they stood drinking their coffee, watching the sun peek up through the trees.

"Noah, I made up my mind last night after you left. Right through them trees behind us, where June is buried, there's about two hundred acres of open land, with a nice little spring running around it. Be a good place to raise some cotton."

He looked down, "I can't leave here. Them kids don't want to leave their mother here alone. So I guess we will just settle right here. I might be makin' a big mistake, but, well," he paused, "that's the way it's gonna be."

Noah looked around, "Probably couldn't do much better elsewhere. I wish you all the best."

"I thank ya for that."

"I think we'll be movin' on. Probably first thing in the mornin'," said Noah.

"Well ole boy, I do hope the best for you folks."

Noah led the way as the Bakers left the Nelson family. They all waved goodbye to each other. "We makin' good time," said Noah, as Bud rode up alongside him.

"This old road ain't traveled much no more, but it is still in good shape. Most people cross farther down, headin' for Dallas."

They made camp that night. "We cain't be too far from the creek," said Noah. "We gotta cross it and travel down the other side. We'll find it tomorrow, I'm sure."

They were up early, and got underway by daylight. About midday, Noah held his hand up. "Let's rest here. Them horses had a long morning."

They came to the creek late that afternoon. It was about twenty feet wide. Bud stopped the wagon. The water ran over a wide flat rock that was only a few inches under the water. The rock went all the way across the creek. A wagon could cross the creek with no trouble. It served as a dam also. The creek was about four feet deep on the upper side.

"Well folks, soon as we cross this here little creek, we can make camp," said Noah.

"How many days from here to where we are goin'?" asked Jennie.

"Ah, maybe three weeks, maybe four, if all goes well," said Noah.

After they crossed over and went about fifty yards, the road turned left, and headed south. They made the turn and were heading south when the back wheel fell into a hole. The wagon came to stop. Bud stood looking at the back of the wagon. The wheel was laying flat. The spokes were busted. The hub was broken and so was the axle.

Noah stood beside his brother in law. "Damn the bad luck," he said.

"Yeah, damn the bad luck is right," said Bud.

Everybody watched as Bud and Noah inspected the damage. Bud walked back toward the creek.

"He's got a lot of thinking to do," Jennie said.

"Yeah, a lot," said Noah. "We cain't fix that axle."

Mary walked back and forth wringing her hands, "What now, what can we do now?"

"Calm down, mama," Jennie said "Paw will think of something, you'll see."

They made camp. Bud and Noah did a lot of talking. The next morning, they unloaded the wagon, then jacked it up off the ground. When the hub came up off the wheel, Bud pulled it out and stood it up. He froze, then he pushed the wheel away, and let it fall back to the ground. He grabbed his chest and looked around, then fell face down.

Nobody moved at first. Then Jennie ran over and knelt down, "Paw." Noah knelt down beside her. He put his hand on Bud's chest. He looked at Jennie.

"Jennie girl, I don't think he can hear you."

"What are you sayin'?"

"He's dead, yore paw is gone."

"But that can't be."

Mary walked slowly to his body. She just stared down at her husband. "You can't just leave us like this. You brought us all this way. Now you are going to just leave us. No, I say, no, no, no."

She turned her face toward the sky. "Lord, what are you doing? This ain't fair."

"Mama," Jennie said, "get a hold of yourself."

Rob took his mother, and walked her over to the front of the wagon and sat her in a chair. "Mama, dad is gone, do you understand?"

"Yes, I understand. I understand that we are out here in the middle of nowhere, with a broke down wagon, and it's all his fault."

Patty came and took her mother's hand. Tears ran down Patty's face. They were all in shock, and disbelief. Noah covered the body with a blanket.

"It doesn't seem real," said Jennie, "it is like a nightmare. I shake my head but it doesn't go away."

Mary never left the wagon, she didn't cry. She just sat in her chair and mumbled to herself. Nobody did much of anything that day. Mostly cried and tried to comfort each other. It was a long night for the Baker family.

"I keep expecting him to get up and come over here and ask for a cup of coffee," said Jennie.

CHAPTER 3

As the sun peaked up over the horizon, it cast light on the Baker camp. They were all wrapped in blankets, sitting around their mother asleep.

Noah opened his eyes. He slept on the ground, with his saddle for a pillow. He sat up, and rubbed his face. 'It is going to be a pretty day. Too bad we got to bury Bud. Them kids been sittin' there asleep, by her chair all night.'

"It is a sad sight to see alright. Damn, I shore do hate to wake 'um up. Think I will stoke up this fire and get me some coffee goin'. They can wake up on their own."

Bud sat by the fire with a cup of coffee and a cigarette. He had a blanket over his shoulders.

The sun was coming up over the trees. He saw Jennie moving. "It won't be long now," he thought. "They will all be awake here soon. Boy, I shore ain't lookin' forward to this day."

Jennie opened her eyes and looked over at Noah. He put his finger to his lips and shook his head. "Let her sleep." He said in a low voice.

Jennie got to her feet and joined Noah. She didn't talk, she poured herself some coffee, and pulled the blanket up over her shoulders.

"A cool tint in the air this morning, but as soon as that sun gets up, it will warm up quick," said Noah.

Jennie tried to control herself but she couldn't hold back the tears. Noah didn't say anything, he just let her cry. Soon all the children were sitting around the fire. They didn't talk. They just sat there staring into the fire. Finally, Noah spoke up.

"Well boys, I hate to have to say this, but we got to get busy. We have to dig a grave. The sooner we get this over with the better."

Rob and Ted stood before Noah with their shovels, "Where do we dig?" asked Rob. Noah called Jennie and Patty over. "We need to pick out a place to dig the grave." They stood there looking around. Jennie crossed the road. She walked down close to the creek. "I say right here, right here next to this creek. What do y'all think?" Rob joined her. "Yep, I think paw would agree."

They stuck their shovels in the ground. Their mother woke up. She walked over to her husband's body. She didn't speak, just stood there, with a blank look on her face. Jennie put her arm around her mother. Finally, Mary returned to her chair and sat down. When Rob and Ted finished the grave, they all pitched in and placed the body in the ground.

"Mama," Jennie said, "come, we are ready to bury paw." Mary sat there with that blank stare, with no expression.

"Mama," said Jennie. "Mama," she said louder. Mary looked up at her daughter. "Nobody told me."

"Told you what?" Mary didn't answer.

"Mama, told you what?" Mary just sat there.

"Come with me Mama. Get up."

"Leave me be." Noah walked up.

"She won't get up, what's wrong with her."

"Maybe she is in shock or something. I have no idea. Let her sit there. She will come out of it sooner or later. Let's get this over with."

They stood there looking at the fresh dirt. "As soon as I get the time, I will make a good head maker," said Rob.

"That will be nice." Said Jennie.

Noah turned and looked around. "Damn, what a mess we got ourselves into. What a mess I got us into. Boy, am I sorry I ever brought this whole thing up to Bud. Too late to cry over spilt milk."

Noah rode up on his saddle horse, "I'll be back, gone take a ride and look around." Jennie and Patty cleaned the breakfast dishes. She told the boys to round up the horses and cows.

"Herd them in closer to camp, we don't need them to get scattered all over the countryside."

Jennie tried to talk to her mother, but all Mary would say is, "we gone die out here, and it's your father's fault. I want to go home."

Jennie walked to the back of the wagon. She looked at the grave, then her mother.

"My paw is dead and my mother has lost her mind, and now she won't eat. Thank God for Uncle Noah."

She sat down on the ground. It was like the whole world was caving in on her. She felt like digging a hole, climbing in and pulling the dirt in on top of her. She sat alone with her thoughts. She was brought back to reality when Noah rode up on his horse.

He dismounted and tied the horse to the wagon. He reached his hand down to her. She took hold and stood up.

"Uncle Noah, what we gone do about maw? She done lost her mind."

"Mary never was the strong one, she got her strength from yore paw. Now that he's gone, well, I guess she just don't know how to handle it."

"What can we do to help her?"

"Only time can answer that question." Jennie looked at her uncle. "I think maybe we should do what the Nelsons did."

He broke out in a smile. "Jennie girl, you amaze me. That's exactly what we need to do. That is all we can do, for now anyway. We can make us a home here. For now, anyway. It's got water, good grass, plenty of trees. We got enough things in that wagon to get us through until we get settled in." She talked it over with her brothers and sister. They all agreed.

"What about mama?" asked Rob.

"I will answer that," said Noah. "No need to say anything to her. Not till she comes back to herself."

They sat and listened to their uncle, "It ain't going to be easy, but with a little hard work, we can make it here for a while. One thing is for sure. If things don't work out here, you kids are still young. You can start over somewhere else."

Jennie spoke up, "We will stick together, work hard and pray. Want be no grumbling, no complaining, everybody doing their share. We are going to make a go of it right here." Jennie looked at each of them. "If it is meant for us to stay here, and for this to be our new home, we will make it. I just feel it."

"Me too," said Rob. Noah got to his feet, "Well, what about you Ted? You ain't said a word bout none of this."

"What if somebody comes along and helps us to move on," said Ted.

"The odds of that are slim and none boy. If somebody does come this way, they will have all they can do to haul their own stuff. Plus, it will take money for us to go anywhere. Money we ain't got."

Without looking up Ted said, "Well, I am grieved about paw, and I worry about mama. I will do whatever ya'll do. I ain't too crazy 'bout leavin', here and nobody to take care of paw's grave." Noah nodded, "Well said."

Jennie put her arm over Ted's shoulder. "I am with you Ted. It just would not be right."

"Let's get to work," said Rob. The first thing we need to do is take the wagon apart. It will be useful to us."

They took the wagon apart. When Rob lifted the water barrel, he found a leather bag. He opened it, and found his father's money. "I figured we would find it, once we took this wagon apart," said Noah. Rob counted the money, "seventy-eight dollars."

"That ain't as much as I figured," said Jennie.

"We had to spend more money than yore paw and me figured on."

"Well no matter, we gon' need every penny of it," said Noah.

"You take it Jennie. Hang on to it," Said Noah.

They unloaded the wagon. Then took the bed off the axels and put two runners on the bottom side. Then hooked one of the horses to it, and used it to haul their things about three hundred yards to the tree line. There was a big shade tree there. Noah decided it would be a good place to build a cabin. A grassy knoll, that ran parallel to the creek. The back side sloped about a quarter mile, down to a streamed. The stream ran around the end of the ridge. It was lined with trees. So, they had a big pasture with good grass for the livestock.

After getting everything moved, they started working on some temporary lodging. They cut small trees and built a frame, then stretched tarps over it. They built one for the boys and one for the girls. They built another one to keep their things dry.

Noah got Rob and Ted started cutting saplings to build a corral for the horses, and one for the milk cows.

"What about the beef cows?" asked Rob.

"We'll keep them close for awhile, but they will be fine out there in the pasture."

"Uncle Noah, do ya think we can make a go of this?"

"Shore we can. But it will take time and hard work."

Noah could see the worry, and the doubt in his eyes. For now, they were full thoughts about staying here, and making this their new home. As for him, he had no idea what the future would hold for them. Maybe it will work out. Maybe this will be their new home. Their future. Only time will tell. For now, it was good therapy. It took their minds off Bud's death, and all the bad luck that had fell on them.

"Rob, it has been done before. It'll be done again, and by us. We don't have much of a choice, not for now. We can't go back. We can't go forward. We got to make it through the winter." He put his hand on Rob's shoulder. "We'll take it one day at a time Rob. One day at a time."

CHAPTER 4

Jennie woke up at her usual time, the sun was just coming up. Patty sat up in her bed. "Jennie, where is momma?" Jennie turned up the lantern. Their mother's bed was empty. She went outside. Her mother was nowhere to be found. Jennie woke Noah.

"I can't find mama."

"Let's don't panic, she has to be around here close."

He got the boys up, they all started looking. After about thirty minutes they came back, one at a time. They all had the same story.

"This doesn't make sense," Rob said. Patty started to cry,

Jennie put her arms around her, "We'll find her sis, don't worry."

They continued to search for their mother. At noon, Jennie and Patty returned to camp. Jennie started a fire and put on some coffee, then started breakfast. She knew the boys would be hungry. She was hoping, when they returned, to see her mother with them. She was disappointed to see them come back without her.

After he ate, Noah saddled his horse. "I will be back by dark," he said.

"Uncle Noah, please find her," Jennie said.

"I'll find her. Nobody can disappear like that. She is too weak to go far."

He crossed the creek and went back toward the Nelson's. He rode at a fast pace for a couple of miles. Finally, he stopped. "No way she could have walked this far." He got off his horse, and lead him over to a tree and tied him to a limb. He sat down. Now he was really worried. "I hate to go back to those kids, and tell them I didn't find their mother."

Noah rode into camp. He dismounted, and stared into their faces. All he could do was shake his head. Their bodies all sagged at the same time. Patty turned and walked away. Noah went to the fire and sat down. Jennie brought him a cup of coffee.

"I'll take care of your horse," Rob said.

"What now?" Jennie asked.

"I just don't know Jennie girl. Not even a sign, nothin'."

Every day, Noah rode out, but it was always the same, nothing. Finally, they all agreed it was hopeless. It was like their mother had vanished into thin air. Tears ran down Jennie's face, "I know she is probably dead. The thought of her laying out there somewhere," she stopped, her head dropped.

Noah reached over and put his hand on the back of her head, "I know, I think about that myself." He looked at each one of the children. "Listen to me. This may not make much sense to you now, but the woman that walked away from here that night, was not the same woman that raised you kids. I know it doesn't make it better. If she was in her right mind, she would never leave you out here like this."

"It's not knowing," said Rob.

"That may haunt us for a long time," said Noah. Rob looked at his uncle, "It will be a long time for me."

The next morning at breakfast, Noah told Rob and Ted to start a garden. "I know it's late but, we got to get something planted. When the weather cools down, we can plant some turnip greens. The cool weather is good for greens."

The grass made it difficult. It took longer than they expected. "This grass is tough," said Rob. "I ain't never seen nothin' like this back home, but I think we got it good enough to plant."

Noah built himself a small lean-to. "I need my privacy," he said.

"One day we will build a house with rooms," Jennie said.

"Yes we will, you can count on it," Noah said. "But for now, I am proud of you kids. You done a man sized job here. Now I think we need to take a few days off and do nothin'."

"Hell yeah," said Rob.

"Boy! that ain't no kind of talk," said Jennie. Noah let out a big laugh.

Jennie tried to hold back a smile, then she busted out laughing. They all started laughing. It was the first big laugh they had in a long time and it felt good.

Spring came early. They found themselves with six little calves and four little horses. Both the milk cows gave birth, both were bulls.

"When they get big enough, they will be beef for the table," said Noah. Noah was glad to see the young calves, that will be a good start to build a herd. He knew the boys wanted to raise cotton, but cattle will be their future. Rob started turning more ground. He wanted to plant more corn this year. He looked out over the land. "One day we will plant cotton," Noah saddled his horse and put a rope on one of the work horses. He was ready to go find the nearest store.

"I hope you won't be gone too long," Jennie said.

"If I am right, there is a store south of here, I just can't remember how far. Don't matter, we need supplies."

Noah had lived ten years in Texas. All of that time was spent south of here around Austin. He and Albert Nelson came this way on their way home.

Every day Jennie would take a break from her chores. She would stand in the shade of the big oak tree and stare down the creek road, hoping to see her uncle returning with good news. Today Patty joined her. They stood in silence for a while.

"I shore do hope he didn't come to no harm," Patty said.

"Don't even think about it. Lord, I hate to think what would happen to us without Uncle Noah. We lost our father, then mama. Losing Uncle Noah would be the last straw."

"It has been four days now," Patty said.

"I know, believe me, I know."

That night at supper, Jennie said the blessing. Before she said amen, she asked that their uncle have a safe journey and return soon. It was followed by three more amen's. Rob broke the plow that morning. He stood up, "Well, ain't no fixin' that thing."

He unhitched the horse and lead him back to the corral. Jeannie could tell something was wrong. Rob had a way of walking when he was upset. She decided to leave him alone, at least till he settled down a bit. Instead, she walked out to the oak tree. After about thirty minutes, Rob joined her. He told her about the plow.

"I don't know about raising cotton on this ground," he said.

Jennie didn't look at him. Her thoughts were down the road, wondering where her uncle was. Rob pointed, "Look, that has got to be Uncle Noah." They watched the wagon as it got closer to them.

"It is," said Jennie, "It is."
"Well Jennie, I think our uncle is home."

CHAPTER 5

It was like Christmas for the Bakers. Jennie and Patty went through the sacks. Jennie sat back in her chair. "We got sugar. We got salt. We got coffee." Rob laid another sack on the table. "We got bacon too."

"Boy, we gonna eat good tonight," said Ted.

"Rob, you and Ted come outside with me." Rob stood by the wagon, it was a small buck board.

"Is this the biggest wagon you could find?"

"It's the only wagon I could find."

"How far is that town?" Rob asked.

"Ain't no town, just a store. Owned by a Mr. Alto. Nice fella. I remembered it, soon as I saw it."

Alto Remo's wagon broke down just like the Perry's wagon. It was full of supplies. He was coming from Louisiana, heading to Dallas to sell them to the local merchants. Lucky for him he had crossed the creek and had gone about fifty yards. The wagon broke down under a big oak tree.

There was a lot of people traveling west. Before long, he had sold everything. He hitched a ride on a freight wagon back to Louisiana. There he bought another wagon and filled it with supplies. When he crossed the creek, he stopped where his wagon had broken down before. With so much traffic going by on their way to Dallas and places west, he sold out fast. He decided to settle there and build a trading post.

It wasn't long till some cowboys showed up. He found out that there were two big cattle ranches nearby. People would stop and camp under the oak tree. Breaking down here was his lucky day.

"It ain't far, only a good day's ride from here. I would have been back sooner but we had some work to do on that wagon."

"At least we got a place to buy supplies," said Rob. Jennie nodded, "Amen to that."

Noah handed him a sack filled with corn seed. "Here, I figured you might need some more of these." Rob grinned, "I broke the plow this morning."

"Well, I reckon we will just have to make another trip to that store, and get us a new one. It's for sure. We gotta have one." Jennie stood with her hands on her hips.

"Well, you done good uncle, you even got us some bacon." Noah had his saddle pony tied to the back of the wagon. There were two sacks tied together, hanging across his saddle.

"Boys, we need to build us a chicken coup, we got live birds here." Jennie put both hands on one of the sacks.

"There's chickens in here boys." They all pitched in and hastily built the chicken coup. "Well," Noah said, "it ain't purty but it will do till we can do better." Patty watched the chickens walking around in their new home.

"If that ole rooster does his job; we should have some baby chicks running around here soon." Jennie blushed, she looked at Noah. He had a big grin on his face.

"Patty!"

"Well, it's true."

"Maybe so, but we don't talk about them things." Embarrassed by her sister, Jennie walked to the house. Patty looked at her uncle. Still smiling, Noah put his arm around Patty's shoulder, "Don't worry Patty girl, she'll grow up one of these days."

The Bakers ate good that night. After supper, they all sat on the porch. "Nice breeze," Jennie said.

"Yep, a real nice night all around," said Noah. "I am shore glad to be home." Jennie looked at her uncle. "Home, sounds strange. I guess this is home for us now."

"Home is where ya hang yore hat," Noah said.

"I think I am going to like it here," said Patty. Noah looked at Ted, "What about you little fella?"

"So far so good." Noah let out a big laugh. They all laughed.

A few days later, Noah took Rob to Mr. Alto's store. They bought the only plow he had. Rob and Ted got busy with the planting. It was a slow process. Rob didn't want to break the new plow. As soon as they got enough ready, Jennie and Patty helped put the corn seed in the ground. As soon as they got the corn planted, Rob and Ted started breaking ground for a vegetable garden. They had plenty of seed their father brought from Alabama. Noah saw Rob leading the horse back toward the barn. He spurred his horse and caught with him.

"What's wrong?" he asked.

"Busted that plow. I think I can fix it," Rob said. "I tried to baby it, but it broke anyway." Noah could see the aggravation on his face.

"It's this grass, this damn grass."

"Yeah, you right. We ain't got the right stuff to farm this land," said Noah.

"We will do the best we can, with what we got." Noah smiled, "We ain't got much choice."

"Just do the best ya can boy, that's all we expect out of you. I'm mighty proud of you boys. Be patient, be patient."

They built a bigger and better chicken pen. The hens were laying eggs and hatching babies. "We will be ok in the egg department," said Patty.

"Yeah, and fried chicken ain't bad either," said Ted.

Noah led his horse out of the corral. Jennie was outside the shack. He mounted up and rode over and stopped, "Where ya headed?"

"Think I will go see if them Nelsons are still here, or maybe they done left and went back home."

"They don't know we are here. If they did stay, they need to know that we are here too." He knew he had to be getting close. He could smelt smoke. "Got to be them Nelson's," he thought.

When he got closer, he saw his friend and boys dragging a log toward their cabin. Noah stopped, "man, they have been busy alright." He could see a log cabin, a barn, a corral with a pole barn. They had cleared about two acres there in the trees. When Albert spotted Noah, he stopped working and came out to greet him.

"Well, well, I see you are back. Where you headed now?"

Noah dismounted, "That's a long story." The two shook hands.

"You just give them reins to my son there, he will take care of that horse for you." They walked up to the house and sat down at a table on the front porch.

"Well, you tell me all about it, over a drink of some good homemade whiskey." They sat with a jug of whiskey between them. After a few minutes of small talk, Noah looked around.

"Makin yore self a nice place here, Albert."

"We will have cotton in the ground next year. We been workin' on this cabin and that barn mostly. Now that it is done, we can spend time on breakin' more ground. We got about five acres of corn planted, and a vegetable garden."

"I done told you what we been doin', now you tell me what you been doin'. And why you are here. 'Cause I shore never expected to be seeing you no time soon." Noah told him what happened after they left them.

"You tellin' me, ya'll been livin' there all this time?"

"Yep."

"Well I be dog gone."

Noah told them about Bud and Mary, how she just vanished. Albert went into his cabin, when he came back, he handed him a ring. Noah looked at it, "Damn, it's Mary's ring, where did you find this?"

"My boys were hunting, they found some bones, this ring was around one of the fingers." Noah sat back in his chair with his chin on his chest. He sat staring at the ring in his hand, "Poor Mary."

"We was curious about who it was, and how they got here. We figured they must have been there a long time. We never even considered it bein' one of you folks."

Still staring at the ring Noah spoke. "After her husband died, well, she just lost it. She just snapped. One night, she walked away. We searched for several days." He looked up at Albert. "We knew she was dead. We kept looking, but it was always the same, no sign, just nothin'. I never figured she would come this far, never."

"I'm terribly sorry 'bout all ya bad luck."

"I am just glad you found her."

"We buried the bones." Noah sat in silence for a few minutes.

"I think I will take them bones back with me. We will bury her next to Bud, her husband. Them kids will want that."

"Tomorrow, I will send my sons after the remains. We will make a coffin and line it with a blanket, then nail it shut. No need openin' it. You can use my wagon. I will send Al with you. He can bring the wagon back home. And we will know where you are."

Noah sat on the wagon seat. He looked at his friend, "Albert," he paused, "I don't know how to thank you for all this."

"No thanks necessary."

"Albert, if I knew then, what I know now."

"I know how you feel, losing my wife. You cain't look at it that way Noah. Ain't no blame goes to nobody."

"If anybody knows, it's you." Albert put his hand on Noah's arm, "Look ahead. It's all up ahead."

Noah nodded. He looked at Al, "Let's go boy. Might as well get this over with."

Noah knew this was going to be a sad reunion. He was glad he could take Mary's remains home. He was sad at how she had died. "It ain't gone be good."

When Noah stopped in the yard, Rob came out to greet him.

"Where did you get the wagon?" he asked.

"This here is Al Nelson. You remember the Nelsons."

"Shore I do," said Rob as he shook hands with Al. He stood looking at the box, "What's that?"

"I found yore maw, Rob."

"You tellin' me she is in that box?"

"Yep."

Rob stood there, staring. Jennie and Patty joined them. They asked the same questions. Nobody spoke, it's like they were frozen. Jennie slowly lifted her head and looked at Noah.

"This is my mama?"

"Yes," he paused. "Yes it is."

"Are you sure?"

Noah reached in his shirt pocket and took out the ring. "Here," Jennie took it in her hand. They all looked at it. Jennie started to cry. It was a loud cry. "Mama," she yelled out.

Noah was not surprised at their reaction. It was what he expected. That's why he was not looking forward to this moment. He told them they would bury her in the morning. That night they sat looking at the wagon. Noah told them how the Nelson's found her.

The next morning after they buried their mother. They said goodbye to Al. "We are glad for all you done," said Jennie. Noah was glad to get it all over with. He was glad these kids could see their mother's grave next to their father. Now they could close that sad chapter of their life, and move on.

CHAPTER 6

The ground was good to them. The corn did well, and the garden made plenty of vegetables. They had over thirty chickens now. They were glad to be having eggs for breakfast and fried chicken for Sunday dinners.

When the weather got cold enough, Noah and the boys dressed one of the steers. The beef was a change in their diet. A welcome change for Noah.

Spring came early. They were all glad of that. The shack they built was drafty and leaked. "We gonna make some improvements to the shack before winter comes this year," Rob said. He got some amends to that.

Jennie and Noah rode around the farm, they counted ten new calves. "That gives us twenty cows," Jennie said.

"It does, four of them little ones are steers. I think we will take them to the store, maybe we can sell or trade them for supplies."

Mr. Alto agreed to buy all the cows and horses they wanted to sell. That was good news to Jennie. It gave them a market. Now they could buy and sell.

"How much will we get for them cows?" asked Jennie.

"Normally, range cows bring about three dollars a head. Them cows you got ain't normal."

"They are way better cows. Got more meat on 'um. I bet they came from back east."

"Yes sir, we brought them from Alabama," said Jennie.

"You think about getting' some of these range cows and cross breed."

"That is something to think about," said Noah.

"Tell ya what I'll do. I will trade you five range cows for one of yore bulls. How 'bout that?"

Noah looked at Jennie. "Jennie girl, that is a good deal."

"Well, ok, deal." Mr. Alto extended his hand, "Shake on it."

"Now that is settled. We need to sell the ones we brought today," said Noah. Mr. Alto rubbed his chin, he looked like he was giving it serious thought, "I'd say five dollars. How does that sound?"

"Pretty good I say," answered Jennie, with a big grin on her face. Mr. Alto looked at Noah. "You folks need to name that ranch of yores, make up a brand."

"Guess it will be the Baker ranch. As for the brand, it'll be the circle B," said Noah. He looked at Jennie, "How 'bout that Jennie girl?"

"Sounds good to me."

A few months later, Noah, Rob and Ted took Mr. Alto a young bull, and brought five cows back to the ranch. With the added cattle, the herd multiplied. And so did the horses. With that, the workload grew also. Jennie turned the cooking over to Patty. She was a good housekeeper, and everybody loved her cooking.

They broke three saddle ponies that year. Noah took them to the store. He bought rifles and pistols. He taught the Bakers how to shoot. They learned quickly.

Jennie learned to shoot and ride. She learned to rope and brand, and make steers out of young bulls. She made a good ranch hand. Noah and Jennie sat their horses, looking at the herd of cattle. "It's been almost five years," Jennie said.

"Don't seem like it," said Noah.

"Jennie, we should have maybe fifteen steers to sell this year. At five dollars a head, that will be about seventy-five dollars."

"That will be a good pay day," said Jennie.

"Yep, and if things keep goin' good, it will get better."

"Poor Rob," said Jennie. "I think he has given up on cotton."

"It ain't his fault," said Noah. "It's this land. We ain't set up to grow a big crop like cotton. Cows, this will make a good ranch. Cattle will do good here. We will have three saddle ponies and four work horses to sell. That's about a hundred dollars. Do you realize how much money we talking about?"

"Yes, and I know that the work is getting to be more than we can handle."

"We can manage for a while yet. Now that Rob ain't trying to farm, he can spend more time working the ranch part. But eventually, we will have to think about hiring some help."

After selling their cows and horses that year, they bought enough lumber to build a new house. With enough rooms for everybody and a big front porch. The Bakers and the Nelsons became good friends. They would get together two or three times a year, and all would have a good time. Al, Albert's oldest son, was sweet on Patty. Al came to Noah and asked to marry her.

"Boy, you asking the wrong person. Jennie and Rob are who you need to talk to. As for me, you got my permission."

Jennie looked at Al, she was pleased that he wanted to marry her sister. He was a hard worker, and basically an all-around good man. She turned to Rob, "what do you say?"

"I don't see why not, do you?" Jennie hugged Al's neck, "No, I don't."

There wasn't a preacher around, so Mr. Nelson and Jennie held a bible while Al and Patty placed their hands on it and said their vows.

"I say these two are married," said Albert, "and I will kill any man that says they ain't." Jennie grinned, "Amen."

Jennie and Rob watched Al and Patty ride back to their new home. "Well, there goes your cook," Rob said.

"Yes, and I am glad for her, I think they will be happy."

CHAPTER 7

The next year brought more changes. Jennie bought a new bull. And to her surprise, Rob announced his engagement to Annie, Albert's daughter. It caught her by surprise. They got married two months later.

Annie was a lovely girl. She fit right in the Baker family. Rob did not move out. He said their house was big enough for all of them, especially since Patty left. Annie took over the cooking and house duties. Jennie was glad. She didn't like house work and Annie did, so all was good.

Noah and Ted sat down at the table. It was the first meal Annie cooked. They ate a little of their food. Ted smiled, he looked at his uncle and nodded. Noah nodded back.

"Well Ted, what do ya think?"

"I think this is a big improvement over what we been eating since Patty left. Maybe now we can start gaining some of our weight back."

"You talking about my cooking?" Jennie asked.

"I think yore cooking can talk for its own self," said Ted. Noah let out a laugh. He almost got choked.

With Rob and Ted working full time, Jennie's workload got a little easier. Noah wasn't able to put in the same work days now. His arthritis was getting bad. He was not able to stay on a horse for long. So Jennie told him to spend more time around the house and help Annie with her chores.

Noah sat on the front porch in his rocking chair. Lately he spent most of his day sittin' on the porch with a jug of Albert's whiskey by his chair. He looked down the road. He saw riders coming. They rode up to the house.

"Howdy," he said.

A tall young man wearing a star on his vest dismounted and walked up to the porch. He removed his hat, "My name is Ben Adams, Texas Rangers."

"Glad to meet ya," said Noah. "How can I help ya?"

"Could we rest here a spell, and if you can spare it, some of that well water would be good. We been drinkin' creek water for the last two months."

"Shore you can. Help ya self. Did you fellas come by the Nelson farm on yore way?"

"No sir, we been chasing some outlaw's north of here. We caught up with them a week ago. Now, we headin' back to Dallas. I didn't know this road was here, we found it about two miles back."

"That explains it," said Noah. "The Nelson farm is more like fifteen miles from here. Are you boys in a big hurry?"

"No sir, right now we too tired to get in a big hurry."

Noah went into the house, he asked Annie if there was anything she could cook up fast. "I got some eggs and I got some biscuits left from breakfast. I can fry up some side meat and gravy."

"Sounds good, we got eight hungry Texas Rangers outside."

"I know, I seen 'um through the screen door. Won't be no problem. I'll call ya when it gets done."

Jennie rode up into the yard. She was surprised to see the men sitting on the porch. They were surprised to see her. She wore a pair of jeans that were a little tight and one of Ted's shirts, that was too small. Her breast pushed the shirt to its limits. The rangers just stared at this good looking woman standing in front of them.

"Jennie, we got company," said Noah.

"I can see that," she said.

She looked down at her clothes, 'no wonder they are staring', she thought. It was close to wash day. She didn't have any clean clothes, so she had borrowed some from Ted. Ted was slim, he and Jennie were about the same height, but Jennie was definitely bigger in her chest and hips.

"Excuse me," she said and went into the house. She dug around in her dirty close, she found some that weren't too bad, "Oh well, these will have to do, for now." She helped Annie in the kitchen, then carried the food out, and set the table.

The rangers ate like they were starving to death. Jennie sat on the front porch with Noah. Ben came out of the house. He rubbed his stomach, and with a big grin, he thanked them for the meal.

"Recon, we made pigs of ourselves. But the food was good and we ain't had no home cookin' in a while."

"No apology needed here son. Glad to help you fellas out. A good meal is the least we could do."

Jennie looked him up and down. He was the handsomest man she had ever seen. And he was dashing in his jeans, his red shirt and blue bandana. He wore high top boots, and a wide brim hat. He had two pistol belts around his waist. She blushed when she realized he was staring at her. She quickly averted her eyes. Lord, he must think I am awful. A woman with no shame.

"I still want to thank you folks. That meal hit the spot. I know them boys liked it."

"Annie done most of the work," Jennie said. Annie came out and sat down next to Jennie, "Them rangers said they wanted to clean up for me." Jennie watched Ben as he mounted up and rode away.

"He shore is a nice looking fella, ain't he," said Annie. Jennie walked off the porch. "I got work to do."

"Ha, she ain't foolin' me," said Annie and went back into the house. Noah grinned, young folks, he thought.

Time past off fast. The herd was growing. It was round up time. Jennie and Ted sat their horses looking down at Rob, who was riding toward them.

"How many do you think we will have this year?" asked Jennie.

"Maybe about 200," he said.

"At five dollars a head, that's a thousand dollars."

"That is a lot of money," she said.

"Never figured we would ever make that kind of money."

"Uncle Noah was right to talk us into coming here. For a while, I sorta blamed him for our parent's death. I kept thinking that if we had stayed in Alabama, they would still be alive. But it was just meant to be. Wasn't nobody's fault."

Ted nodded, "Me too, guess we all thought that way at first." Rob rode up alongside them. "I am glad we stopped farming. I think we will do better with these cows."

"This is cattle country," said Noah. "Some parts of Texas may be good for cotton."

Rob and Jennie talked to Mr. Alto about buying their cows. He told about a buyer in Nacogdoches. "He will pay more than I can. I plan to drive about a hundred or so down myself. I got some drovers hired. If you folks want to join them herds together and team up with them drovers, you are welcome."

It was a three-week trip. Everybody went. They wanted to do some shopping in a real town. Everybody but Noah. He didn't want to make the long trip. So he decided to stay and feed the livestock. Jennie didn't figure it would take that long. She knew cows walked slow, but not this slow.

"Damn these cows walk slow."

"You done said that a hundred times," said Rob.

"And it is true." Rob grinned. His sister was impatient alright.

It was a long hard trip. Not what they expected. The drovers were a big help. At the end of the drive, Jennie walked up to the trail boss. "I just want to thank you so much for all you and your men did for us. I doubt that we would be here now if not for you."

They separated the two herds outside of town. When the buyer came and looked over the Baker's cows, he offered Jennie ten dollars a head. The tally was one hundred and eighty head. They lost almost twenty cows on the drive. Jennie signed the bill of sale. The buyer gave Jennie a check for one thousand eight hundred dollars. Annie and Jennie did a lot of shopping, mostly for new clothes.

"I ain't had this much fun before," said Annie.

"We ain't never had this much money before."

The men bought new saddles and new pistols. Rob bought a wagon. "We will need it to carry all this stuff back home," he told Jennie. They stopped at Alto's store on the way home and spent the night there. A Mexican family was camped there also. Mr. Alto hired them to help around the store. His regular helper broke his arm.

"They are good people, hard workers too," said Mr. Alto. "Make you some good help."

"What about you. I mean how long will you need them here?"

"Ole John will be back in a few days. He will have one arm but he knows what to do. He can get a lot done."

Jennie went out onto the porch. She looked at the Mexican family. 'We could definitely use the help', she thought.

CHAPTER 8

Carlos Santo was born in Texas, so was his wife Maria. Carlos was 40 years old. Maria was 35. They had 3 kids. Jaun 14, Karla 12 and Manny 9. They all spoke English. Jennie found Rob. She talked to him about hiring the Santos family.

"We could use the help, that's for sure."

"We can't pay a lot right now," said Jennie. "But if things keep going good, in time we could do better."

"It won't hurt to ask." Said Rob. "Let's go talk to them."

"Mr. Santo, can we speak to you for a minute?"

"My name is Carlos and yes we can talk."

"I hear your lookin' for a job," Jennie said. Carlos grinned, "Yes ma'am."

They sat and talked for a long time. Jennie liked Carlos and his family. They seemed like very nice people. Carlos had been watching the Baker family. They were nice to his wife and kids. The two families seemed to get along well.

"I know it will be hard to find maybe. I am looking for more than a job. I would like to find a place to settle in and make a home for my family. I am not worried about the money. If this is more than you are looking for, I understand. But I will work for you for a while, but not forever. I hope you understand what I am trying to say."

"I do understand," said Jennie. "If you come to work for us, and you decide to leave, it will be okay."

"If it doesn't work out and we part company, no hard feelings."

Jennie looked Carlos in the eye. He grinned and stuck out his hand. She shook hands with Carlos. "You got a job. Can you be ready to leave here in the morning?"

"Yes ma'am."

Carlos stopped his wagon. He looked around the ranch. "This is a good place Maria. I think we will like this place, and these people."

"I hope so," she said. "We have had no good luck since we left San Antonio."

"This time it will be different. I just feel it." He followed the Bakers up to the house.

Annie was glad to have Maria to help with the housework. She found out Maria was a good cook. It didn't take them long to develop. Jaun was a good horseman, and he was good with cows. He spent his days with Rob and Ted. Carlos took over the vegetable garden. He looked after the chickens and milk cows. Karla and Manny helped their father with his chores, and their mother, when she needed them. There was plenty for everybody to do.

Noah spent most of his day on the front porch, in his rocking chair. His arthritis was getting worse. He kept a jug of Mr. Nelson's whiskey by his rocking chair. He said it helped.

For now, everything was good. Carlos and his family found themselves a home here with the Bakers.

It was early spring, Annie sat on the porch talking to Noah. She looked up the road. "Riders," she said, "probably drifters."

When the riders crossed the creek, instead of turning left and staying on the road, they went straight and came up the drive to the house.

"Recon, they will be asking for a job," said Annie.

"Or a handout," said Noah.

The three men rode up to the porch. One of them had red hair. One was a short and round, the third man was slender, with a long beard.

"What can we do for ya?" Noah asked.

"People call me Red. We would like to see the owner."

"Well ain't none of 'um here right now," said Annie.

"State yore business," Noah said, in a stern voice.

"Red, sounds like that ole man is getting' rude with us," said the little fat man. Red dismounted and started up onto the porch.

"Hold on there fellow. That's far enough. You just get right back on that horse and ride on out of here."

Noah tried to pull his pistol, but his fingers were stiff. All three of the men pulled their pistols and fired at Noah. They fired several shots. Noah dropped his gun and rolled slowly from his chair, dead.

Annie screamed and ran into the house. Red dismounted and followed her. She put up a good fight, but he managed to drag her into the bedroom. He threw her onto the bed. The other two men dismounted and walked up on the porch. The fat man picked up the jug of whiskey. He took a drink, smacked his lips, and with a grin he said, "thanks, ole timer."

Maria was standing in the front room. She ran to the kitchen. "Hey fat boy, looks like we got us a Mex, let's go get her."

"Nah, you go ahead. I'll be there in a minute." He took a drink of the whiskey. The outlaw followed Maria into the kitchen. Maria had a knife.

"I got me a fighter here," he said. He got hold of her arm, and hit her with his fist. Maria went limp. He shook the knife from her hand, then pushed her to the floor. Jennie was only a hundred yards away, when she heard the gunfire. She rode into the yard and saw the strange horses, then she saw Noah's body.

"No, oh no." She ran up onto the porch and knelt down. She had her hand over her mouth. She heard Annie scream from inside. She realized what was happening. Jennie picked up Noah's gun, then pulled her pistol from its holster and walked to the front door. She cocked both pistols. The door was halfway open. Jennie kicked it open with her boot. The fat man stood with the jug to his mouth. When he saw Jennie, he dropped it and reached for his gun. Jennie fired, the bullet hit him in the chest. He fell to the floor, dead.

Red was on top of Annie, trying to get her dress up. He heard the shot and grabbed his gun belt, then went to the door and peeked out. He pulled his gun. Like a cat, Annie rolled off the bed. Rob kept a pistol under the mattress. She ran her hand in and pulled it out. She fired three times. Red turned his face toward Annie.

"You bitch," he said. He took one step, then fell dead in the hall.

Jennie saw a man standing in the kitchen door. He looked down and saw his buddy dead on the floor. Then he looked at Jennie standing there with two pistols in her hands. In haste, he pointed his gun at Jennie. She felt the wind from the bullet as it went by her head. She fired back, but missed. He ran out the back door.

"Maria!" yelled Jennie.

"I am alright." She called out to Annie, "I'm okay."

Shots came from the yard, Jennie went to the front door, then more shots. She looked out the door. Rob was laying on his side, propped up on his elbow.

"Rob," she cried out.

"It's ok Jennie, he's dead." She ran off the porch and over to where her brother lay.

"You been shot."

"Is Annie ok?"

"She's okay, Rob."

"Thank God."

Carlos came riding up, "Maria, where is Maria?"

"In the house, and she is okay," said Jennie. Jennie could see that her brother was in pain.

"Jennie, go check on Annie." Rob said.

"She is fine, it's you that needs attention."

Jennie ran into the house, she grabbed some clean rags and a pan of water and headed back outside. Maria looked at Jennie. "Is somebody hurt?"

"Yes, Rob. He has been shot in the leg."

Maria stood up. Carlos tried to stop her. She told him that she was going to help Jennie. She looked at her husband, "Nothing bad happened to me, Carlos. I got hit in my face, that's all. Now come, Jennie needs us."

When Jennie got back outside, Annie was kneeling down beside Rob. "Let's get him into the house," said Maria. Rob screamed out in pain when they picked up.

It was bedlam at the Baker house to say the least. Carlos, Ted, and Jaun, loaded the bodies in the wagon. Jennie came outside, "Ted."

"What," asked Ted.

"Take 'um far away."

He nodded, "Don't worry, we will."

"Manny," said Carlos. "Take their horses to the barn. Take the gear off of them, then turn 'um out into the corral. Check the saddle bags, see what's in them."

"Yes sir."

Jennie went back into the house. Annie came from the kitchen with a fresh pan of water. Jennie put her hand on Annie's arm.

"Annie, did he…?"

"No, it didn't get that far, thank the Lord."

Maria had treated gunshot wounds before. Jennie was glad she was there. Jennie watch Maria doctoring on her brother. It was a bloody mess. The smell of blood filled the room. It made Jennie nauseated. Maria stood up. She turned and looked at Jennie with a look of helplessness on her face. Jennie motioned for her to come outside.

"What do you think?" asked Jennie.

"The bullet went through his knee cap. That will be a problem for him later. Right now, I got to get the bleeding stopped."

"Are you alright? Did that man hurt you? You know what I mean." Maria shook her head. "No, thanks to you."

Jennie put her arms around Maria. Jennie and Ted went out on the front porch. They covered Noah's body with a blanket.

"I can't believe this; it doesn't seem real. All of it, it's like a bad dream." They both sat there and cried.

"I know, it just ain't right. He never did anybody wrong."

"Look," said Ted, "rider comin'."

Jennie pulled a rifle from Red's horse. She cocked it, then aimed it at the rider. "You can stop and turn around, and get the hell off my land." She aimed over his head and fired, "I mean it, the next one will be lower."

He raised his hands in the air. "Jennie, it's me, Ben Adams, Texas Ranger." She threw the rifle to the ground. "I remember, come ahead."

"What the hell happened here?"

"What does it look like to you?"

Ben pointed at the blanket on the porch. "Who is that?"
"Uncle Noah," she said.

"Ah hell, I hate to hear that."

Maria finally got Rob's leg to stop bleeding. They all hated the one thing that had to be done. Burying their uncle, but it had to be done. They buried him alongside their mother and father. Jennie stood at the foot of his grave.

"So long, Uncle Noah. Thanks for all you did. We will miss you." She turned and walked away.

Ben went back to the house when he left the grave. He wanted to stay awhile. At least, till things settled down. Jennie got out of the wagon. When she walked by Ben, he took hold of her arm.

"I just want to say how sorry I am about all this."

Her lips were quivering. "Why didn't you get here sooner? You could have prevented all of this." She took her fist and beat on his chest. Tears ran down her face, "It's your fault."

Ben put his arms around her, and pulled her against him. She laid her head on his chest and cried. She felt something she had not felt since her father died. She felt safe, secure, it was a good feeling to have his arms holding her.

He put his hand under her chin and lifted her face. He took his bandana and dried the tears from her face.

"I'm sorry," she said, barely above a whisper. She turned and went into the house.

Ben sat by Rob's bed. He wanted to hear the details of what happened. Rob told him how Annie and Jennie had killed the two outlaws.

"Damn, I bet them hombres never expected that," said Ben.

"I bet now they wish they had gone on down the road," Rob said.

CHAPTER 9

It took Maria a few days to get over what had happened, but for Jennie and Annie, they were having trouble getting over the killing part. Jennie and Annie sat on the porch after supper. Ben joined them. Nobody spoke for a few minutes.

"Ben, can I ask you a personal type question? You don't have to answer if you don't want to."

"Sure."

"Well, have you ever killed anybody?"

"Yes," he paused, "I have."

"How do you get over it? Is it easier for men than women?"

"I can't talk for everybody, just myself. I don't think it is easier for men than women."

He sat there with his head down, "You just have to come to terms with it. Those men came here to do harm to you and your family. If you hadn't shot them, you would not be here. You did what you had to do. They didn't give you girls much of a choice."

He sat up straight in his chair and looked at Jennie. "You probably saved some other family from a terrible tragedy."

"It takes a toll on ya, you just put it behind you. Don't think about it, eventually it gets better." He stood up, "I ain't got no more words, Jennie."

"You said enough, I think you have helped us."

"I hope so. I really do." He walked off the porch. "I think maybe I will be leavin' at first light."

"I hope you come back," Jennie said.

"I will be back."

Jennie was up early. She stood looking out the window. She watched Ben lead his horse from the barn. He got up in the saddle and rode by the front of the house. She wanted to run out and tell him goodbye. She wanted to hug and kiss him. All she did was watch him ride away. "You better comeback big boy."

When Patty heard about what had happened, Al brought her to visit. It helped Jennie a lot having her sister there. She took Patty to Noah's grave. "It just don't seem real, Jennie."

They stayed a few days. The Bakers hated to see them go. It was obvious, Rob was going to have a stiff leg. The bullet went right through his kneecap. At times the pain was almost unbearable. Sometimes the only way he could sleep was to drink enough whiskey to pass out. Maria told Jennie to send someone to Alto's store. "He may have something for the pain."

She sent Ted and Manny. They brought back two bottles of laudanum. It worked and Rob was able to rest better. Maria took very good care of him. Rob was glad she was there.

Jennie rode her horse to the top of a rise. There was a big shade tree right on top. She could see a long way, "God, this is some pretty land. I am glad we are here, but it has come at too high a cost. Uncle Noah used to meet me and Rob here. We had some good talks." She hung her head. "I am really going to miss that man. I just thank God he was here to help us." Jennie spurred her horse. "I will be glad when Rob is back on his feet."

Ben walked into his captain's office. He laid his badge on his desk. "I'll be leavin', figured I might as well get it over."

"Is something wrong?"

"No sir."

"What are you planning to do, if I can ask."

"I plan to go to the Baker ranch and ask for a job."

"I know you done give this a lot of thought, so I am not going to try and talk you out of it."

"No sir, I have made up my mind."

"I wish you would take that badge with you. It will be a big help to me, having a man up there to sorta keep an eye on things."

Ben picked up the badge. He held it in his hand. "I guess I can do that." The captain stood up. He shook hands with Ben. "Good luck."

"Thank you."

"Oh, by the way, ain't no pay goes with that." Ben smiled. "I figured that."

"One more thing, there's a war brewing."

"I know, but do you really think it will get that bad?"

"I do, and it will be soon. Ben, when it comes, stay put. We will need you here."

"That won't be hard. I don't even know what it's all about." Ben rode up to the house. He dismounted and tied his horse to the rail.

"Hello," he called out. The door opened slowly. "It's me, Ben Adams." Annie opened the door and came onto the porch. She had a big grin on her face.

"Welcome back, good to see ya."

"Thanks, glad to be here."

"Well, don't just stand there. Come up here and have a seat."

Maria brought some water and a small jug of whiskey. Karla and Manny joined them. They talked for a few minutes. "Can I see Rob?"

Annie stood up, "Come with me." Rob was glad to see him. They had a good visit. "Rob, I come here to ask for a job."

Rob looked up at Ben, "Can I ask what happened between you and the Texas Rangers?"

Ben took the badge from his vest pocket. "I am still with them. I am sorta part time."

"I say yes to the job, but you got to check with Jennie. You might as well know before you start. Jennie is the boss around here."

"I done figured that out."

"Well then, there won't be no trouble there."

Ben heard Jennie talking to Annie. "Guess I might as well get this over with."

She was surprised to see him. Everybody went into the house and left the two of them alone.

"You here on business?" she asked.

"No, I am here on my own business." Jennie didn't say anything.

"I come to ask for a job."

"You want a job here?"

"Yes I do,"

She got to her feet and walked to the end of the porch. Her heart was racing. She didn't want him to see her face. She was breathing heavy. She was sure he could see her heart beating. 'Could I be in love with this man.'

"You don't have to pay me much, I got money of my own."

With her back to him, she said, "If it's alright with Rob. We shore could use the help alright."

She was trying not to sound too eager. She wheeled around and walked fast to the front door. "I will talk to Rob, you wait here."

"Well Jennie, with me laid up like this, he will be a lot of help to you, I like him too. I know you do."

Maria stood in the doorway of Rob's bedroom. "I like him too. We all like him."

"Well there ya go, hire the man," said Rob.

"If you are sure."

"I'm sure," said Rob.

She left the room and went back out onto the porch. Maria smiled, "It would have broken her heart if you had sent him away."

Rob nodded. "I know."

"Rob said for me to hire you, so you got the job."

It was awkward for Jennie, having Ben around every day. She tried to avoid him as much as possible. Rob was getting around better, his leg was straight, it will always be that way. He would hitch up the buck board and ride around the ranch.

"This leg sure is taking a long time to heal," he told Ben.

"At least you can walk. I saw a man that was shot in the knee. It just flopped around. Never could walk on it."

"I am glad to be alive and I can walk. It still hurts when I ride a horse," said Rob.

CHAPTER 10

Jake and Pete Nelson, Alberts two youngest sons, came by. They had a wagon full of homemade whiskey. It was the Nelson family's main source of income. They could raise corn easier than cotton. Albert said, "Cotton will come later." But they kept raising more corn, and making more whiskey.

They spent the night, then left early that morning. Their destination was Miss Jules' place, about ten miles past Alto's store. It was a saloon, with gambling, and whores. The boys would enjoy all three, after they made the sale. They had been there several times before. Pete spent most of the day gambling. He was usually lucky, but this time he was losing his father's money.

Jake came over to the table. He watched the game for a while. "You being cheated, brother," said Jake.

A tall man wearing a white shirt and a tie, leaned back in his chair. "Well young fella, just who would you say is doin' all this cheatin'?"

"You, you doin' the cheatin'," said Jake.

"You better be able to prove that," said the gambler.

"I saw ya, that's enough proof for me," said Jake.

"Not for me it ain't." The gambler stood up and went for his gun.

Jake and Pete pulled their pistols at the same time. All three men started shooting. The gambler had friends. They joined in. When the smoke cleared, the gambler was dead, but so were Jake and Pete.

Miss Jules knew Jake and Pete well. She looked down at their bodies. "I really hate this. They were good boys." She had them loaded into their wagon, she told her two helpers to take them to Alto's store.

"He will see they get home. This will just about kill Mr. Albert."

"Yes ma'am." Mr. Alto had the bodies taken to the Baker ranch. It was almost too much for Annie. Seeing her brothers lying there in the wagon. She could only sit and cry. Ted drove the wagon with the two boys. Jennie drove another wagon with Annie. They left right away.

Albert knew something was wrong when he saw Ted driving his wagon, with Jennie and Annie in another wagon behind them. He walked up the wagon, he looked at the blankets in back. He looked at Annie, she was crying, "Annie, what has happened here?" She tried to talk but the words wouldn't come out. Ted knew it was hard for her to speak.

"It's Jake and Pete."

Albert went to his knees, he held onto the wagon. "No," a long pause, "it can't be, it just can't be."

It devastated the Nelson family. They had to bury them right away. Nobody said very much until after they filled in the graves.

"Ted, my sons were shot, that is obvious. Do you know why?"

"I don't know the reason."

Albert sat on the porch with Ted and Jennie. "This country has been rough on our families. I wish we had never come here."

"Yes it has," said Jennie. "But we are here. It's too late to be looking back. All we can do is move ahead. Go on from here."

Albert didn't say anything, he just sat there and nodded in agreement. Jennie, Ted and Annie left the next morning. Annie hated leaving her father, but she knew Patty would take good care of him.

Ben stood by his horse, tightening the cinch. Rob and Jennie sat on the porch. Ben put his boot into the stirrup, and swung his leg over the saddle.

"I'll be back," he said, "soon as I find out what happened to them boys."

"You take care, we don't need to be burying nobody else," said Jennie.

He grinned. "I plan on comin' back." He looked at Jennie, "I got plans, getting' planted ain't one of them."

Ben talked to Mr. Alto. He told Ben where they went after they left his place. "Them boys been makin' that trip for several years now." Alto looked down at the floor. "Ben, I really hate that them two hade to die so young."

"Yes sir, I agree with you on that," said Ben.

"You goin' down there ain't ya."

"Yes sir, I gotta find out what happened."

"You be careful Ben, that's a rough place alright."

Miss Jules told Ben what happened. "The ones involved in that shootin', they lit out that same day." She said. She put her hand on Ben's arm. "Ain't no tellin' where they are now." Ben realized that would be the end of it. He headed back to the ranch. He told them what he found out.

"Ain't no telling where them fellas are by now," said Ted.

"Well at least we know what happened," said Annie. "That's something."

"I'll be goin' to yore paw's farm in the morning."

Al was going to the field to plow. He wanted to get the ground turned over for winter. Ben saw him, he rode over and told him what he found out.

"I am at least glad to know. Can you tell paw for me?"

"I really don't want to but I will, if you want me too."

"He's up at the house, he ain't done much since we buried Jake and Pete."

"I think knowing will give him some peace. Won't take away the hurt, now he will at least know how it happened, and why." Ben nodded.

It was a cool day, and the wind was blowing. Albert sat in the yard, by a fire. Ben sat down and told him the story. Albert sat with his head down looking at the ground.

"I always told my boys, ain't no good in a deck of cards. But boys don't listen when they are young." He picked up a jug of whiskey and took a drink, then offered Ben the jug.

"This will take the bite out of that wind."

Ben took a drink and gave the jug back to Albert. They shook hands. "Thanks boy, I am glad to know what happened."

Ben left the next morning. He liked the Nelsons, but this time he was ready to leave. Jennie was waiting for Ben. When he got there, Manny took his horse to the barn. He washed up and came to the table, Maria brought him a plate of food. They listened while he told them about his visit.

"Maybe in the spring, we can all go visit them." Jennie said.

"That will be nice." Annie said.

After the spring round up, they took their trip to the Nelson's. Albert was a broken man.

"Jennie, I need to talk to you," said Al.

"Sure, anytime."

"It's kinda private."

"Alright, lets walk."

When they were away from the others, she asked him what he wanted.

"I ain't able to work this farm by myself. Paw ain't much help. It's like he doesn't care no more."

"What do you need from me?"

"Cows, I think I can raise cows easier than cotton. We getting' out of the whiskey business. That was more paw's doing. Now, he won't even go to the still. He said we got enough whiskey already made to last us a long time. He is right about that. Jennie, I would like for you to sell me a few cows? Ranching has been good to your family. I think with a little help, the Nelson family will make out too."

She thought a few minutes. "How would you like to be partners? I will furnish the cows to get you started. You raise 'um 70/30. I get 30%, you get 70%. You got the land and the grass. We'll help you with the roundup and the branding. You can run your cows in with ours and we can drive them to the sell. I'll bring you about 30 or 40 head of brood cows and a good bull. That will be a good start. After two years, we'll split the profit."

"Well, what do you say to that deal?"

"I say hell, yes. How could I go wrong, with a deal like that?" They shook hands.

"If you need some money…"

Al held up his hand. "No, we got enough to get through. Thanks anyway."

"Just the same, if you need anything, well, just let me know."

"I will." He said.

"Promise?"

Al grinned. "I promise."

CHAPTER 11

The next two years were good for Al and Patty. Al was right. Raising cows was easier than raising corn and cotton. Mr. Nelson started taking more interest. Patty gave birth to a baby boy. They named him Jake. And they sold 11 steers to Mr. Alto.

Ted and Jaun came back from Alto's store with bad news. "They went and done it." Ted said. "We are at war. Texas is going to be right in the middle of it."

A few days later some confederate soldiers came to the ranch. They were recruiting for the cavalry. The officer in charge offered Ted and Ben a commission.

"You will be lieutenants in the Texas cavalry."

Ted and Ben joined. Jennie did not try to stop them. She knew it wouldn't do any good. Ted shook Manny's hand, "I reckon you will take my place till I get back."

"Yes sir, I will do my best."

Jennie gave Ted a hug, "Take care of yourself, I'll be expecting you home when this is all over, I love you brother."

"I love you too," he said.

Jennie stepped in front of Ben and stuck out her hand. Ben looked at it, then pulled her to him and kissed her hard on the mouth. Jennie stood there with her arms down by her side. Ben drew back. Jennie opened her eyes and looked into his face. She put both arms around his neck and kissed him back.

"I will be back to get some more of them." Jennie never spoke. The kiss said it all.

Two months later, Al joined up. He was made an officer in the infantry. The confederate army came to the ranch, to buy horses. Jennie sold them at half price.

"That's a good price," said the Major.

Jennie demanded gold and silver. They came back later and bought some beef. Nobody was home that day. So after the soldiers left, Jennie and Rob took all the money they had, and put it on the table. It was all gold and silver. They counted it. Jennie sat back in her chair. "Four thousand six hundred and fifty-five dollars."

"That's a lot of damn money," said Rob.

"Rob, I say we bury most of this money, we don't need it all. We can keep out six hundred."

"Whatever you say."

"Something tells me to hide it."

"We will follow your instincts."

They dug a hole next to the barn. They put the money in two glass jars, wrapped in an oil cloth. "We will leave it there till we need it," said Rob.

When Jennie went to visit Patty, she had a talk with Mr. Nelson. She told him about hiding the money, and how she felt about the future. He told her he felt the same way.

"I will help the confederacy as much as I can, but I intend to take care of my family first. No matter what."

"I feel the same way, and I agree with you on that." Jennie said.

The army came again, and bought more cows and horses, and paid for them with paper money. After three years of war, the south was broke without money. The north had block aides at all the ports. Nothing was coming in or going out. It was only a matter of time now. The south was running out of everything. The armies couldn't keep fighting, with nothing to fight with.

The southern army was suffering some major defeats. With everything going to the army, there was little left for the civilian population. Jennie could see what was happening. They all knew it wouldn't be long till the south would have to surrender. It would be a hard pill for the people to swallow.

She told Carlos and Jaun to keep the cows away from the house and let the horses run wild.

"Just keep them on the ranch," she said.

"Why?" Rob asked.

"Mr. Alto said if we didn't sell the cows to the army, they would just take them. They have already got half our herd. Most of them paid for with paper money. It is worthless. That's alright, I want to help out. But not give up everything. When this war is over, the south will have to start from scratch. The north and the south will need beef. At least I hope so. Maybe we will be able to feed some of them. It won't be easy, but at least we won't be broke, and we will have a few cows left."

"Well, you've been right about things so far, you will probably be right this time."

Annie told Rob he was going to be a 'papa'. They had a son. They named him Noah Martin Baker. That was the only good news that year.

At the end of that year, Al came home. He had been shot in his stomach. He couldn't straighten up. His wound healed on the outside, but not inside. It was a month before he could stand up without pain.

He and Patty sat on the porch watching their son Jake playing in the yard. Patty saw Albert coming toward the house. He was leading a horse with a rider.

"What has paw got there?" Al asked.

Albert stopped the horse, "Give me a hand here Al."

Patty looked at the man, he had a beard, and he was dirty and smelly. He sat with his head down like he was asleep.

"Is he alive?" Patty asked.

The man lifted his head and looked around. He stared at Patty. She gasped and put her hands over her mouth, "Ben!"

He tried to smile. He closed his eyes and fell off the horse. When he opened his eyes, he didn't know where he was. The door opened, Al stuck his head in the bedroom. "Well, I see you are awake."

Ben smiled, "Boy am I glad to see a familiar face."

Al came in and sat down beside the bed. Ben looked under the covers. "I took them clothes and burned 'um. Me and paw washed you off a little. We didn't want to get too personal about that. I figure you can do a better job when you get up."

"Reckon, I was a mess at that."

Al grinned, "Yep, you was at that."

Albert came in with some clothes, "They belonged to Jake. I think they will fit." Ben got a good bath. He sat on the front porch, Patty cut his hair and shaved his beard off.

"Do you know where Ted is and if he is alright?" she asked.

Ben hesitated, "No, I don't." He watched her go into the house.

"Al, Ted is gone. He got shot. I just didn't have the heart to tell her."

Al hung his head, "I hate to hear that. Ted was a good man."

"He was a good soldier, good to his men."

Al took a deep breath. "I'll tell her after you go."

He stayed the next day, he told them that he would be leaving in the morning. "That horse of yore's ain't ready for no saddle. We will give you ole tob, he ain't much, but he'll take you to the Baker ranch."

"I want to thank you for everything."

"We're just glad you made it here."

"I say one thing, I will be leaving in better shape than when I got here."

"You damn shore look better," Albert said.

"Well, I think I will leave on that."

CHAPTER 12

Ben received a hero's welcome. They were all glad to have him back alive. Jennie was especially happy. She ran up to him and jumped into his arms. He held her tight against him. She gave him a big kiss.

He told them how the Nelsons had helped him. They were all full of questions. When they asked about Ted, Ben paused, then broke the bad news. Jennie didn't cry. She sat with her head down. She knew the odds were slim that both of them would get back.

"Do you know how it happened?" asked Jennie.

Ben felt like they should know, so he told them everything. "Things were going bad for us, no food, no ammunition, medical supplies. Hell, some of our men didn't have shoes. How can you ask a man to fight when he has nothing to fight with? Anyway, we got separated from our regiment. Me and Ted had lost so many men, so we joined together. We set out that morning to look for the rest of our company. I had no idea the Yankees were anywhere close to us. Me and Ted were out front of the column. The Yankees ambushed us. My horse got hit, and fell into Ted's horse. When I got to my feet, I saw Ted on the ground. He had been shot through the shoulder. I dragged him to the side of the road. I had to get the men out of there. They had scattered through the woods. I found Sergeant Smith, I told him to get the men out of there. I would catch up with him. I circled back to find Ted. When I found him, he was bleeding bad. There was nothing I could do."

Ben hung his head, "I lost a good friend that day. I found the sergeant. We tried to regroup, but we only found five men that afternoon. That night, I sat looking into the fire. It is hopeless, I told myself. I didn't have the heart to tell those men to stay. We had no powder, no shot, no food. So the next morning, we headed west. Headed home. Nobody spoke. They rode in silence. It might have been wrong for us to leave, but it's over. It's over."

A few days later Ben sat on the porch, talking to Jennie. He watched three confederate soldiers cross the creek and ride up to the house.

"Howdy boys," he said. They were a ragged lot. Dirty and unshaven. One of the men nodded. "Have ya heard? The war is over."

"You mean it? You telling the truth?"

"Yes sir, it's over."

There was a quiet sigh of relief and silence, like a spell fell on them. Ben broke the spell, "You boys look tired and hungry. Them horses look worse. If Miss Jennie don't mind, you fellas join us here on the porch. Maybe we can scrounge up some soap and water, and some clean clothes."

"Sure," said Jennie, "we can do that." She turned to Manny. "Take their horses to the barn. Give 'um some feed, then turn them out into the pasture."

"Maria fed them some beans and cornbread."

They got a hot bath, and some clean clothes.

"Burn them old uniforms," said Ben.

"Ain't much left to burn," said Carlos.

Ben sat on the front porch talking to the three soldiers. Rob brought a jug of whiskey and tobacco onto the porch, and sat them on the table.

"Help yourselves boys, if ya like."

"It'll be a pleasure. We ain't had no whiskey or tobacco in a good while."

They finally got around to introductions. Mason, Rex and Lewis Pitts we're brothers. They owned a small ranch south of Fort Worth. They stayed the night. After breakfast, Mason, the oldest shook hands with Rob.

"We are grateful to you folks. I think we can make it now. I know them horses were glad to get some rest and feed."

"We are glad to help," said Jennie. "And if you boys ever come this way again, stop and visit."

"We shorely will ma'am," said Rex.

Ben watched the men ride away. He was glad to hear that the war was over.

"They never said who won," said Jennie.

"The north," said Ben, as he got to his feet and walked to the edge of the porch.

"Them boys was lucky to make it through alive."

Ben was moody and quiet. He stayed to himself a lot. And they left him to himself.

"He'll work it out," said Rob, "he just needs a little time."

Several weeks went by with no change in him. One morning, Ben left after breakfast. Jennie went to the barn. Carlos helped her saddle her horse. She mounted up and rode out after Ben. Ben stopped on top of the knoll, and sat looking out across the range. Jennie rode up close to him, their knees were touching.

"Beautiful, ain't it?" He turned his head to look at her. "Yep," she said.

She started to speak. Ben put his arm around her waist. He pulled her close against his body, and kissed her hard on the mouth. It took her by surprise. Ben released her and drew his head back from her. Jennie didn't move. She was breathing hard, and if he pulled her from her horse and made love to her right there on the ground, she would do nothing to stop him. He did.

Jennie lay there with her eyes closed. "I had no idea that could feel so good." Ben gave a big kiss on the lips. "I love you," he said.

"If I thought otherwise, you would not have done what you just did." She sat up and started putting her back on. "I say one thing, you picked a helluva place to do this. Right here on the highest place on the ranch. We can be seen for a half a mile in any direction."

"I didn't think about all that," said Ben.

"And I didn't care," said Jennie. "You know you gotta marry me now."

"Yeah, I know. I been thinkin' bout that for a while."

Jennie was busy tucking her blouse in. Ben walked over and put both arms around her waist. She put her arms around his neck. "There will be no more of that till after the wedding."

"I love you, Jennie Baker."

"I love you too."

He kissed her forehead. "This ain't exactly what I imagined when I thought about asking you to marry me."

She smiled. "No, I never thought it would happen like this, but it turned out alright. Pretty good I'd say."

"Ben, I know you went through a lot in that war. And it will be a long time healin'. I want to marry a whole man."

"And you will."

Jennie put her boot in the stirrup. "By the way, I enjoyed that."

Ben blushed a little, "Me too." She swung into the saddle and rode back to the house.

CHAPTER 13

Carpetbaggers came to the ranch. They called themselves tax collectors, and presented Jennie with a bill for a 'X' hundred dollars. They were surprised when she gave them the money and demanded a receipt. Rob watched them ride away.

"They was sure surprised when you gave them that money."

"Ain't you glad we buried that money?"

"You was smart there Jennie, real smart."

They watched the carpetbaggers cross the creek.

"They are going to Al's place now," said Rob. "Them fellas will be in for another surprise."

"Rob, me and Ben are getting married."

"I am glad. He will make you a good husband." He gave her a hug and kissed her forehead. Jennie loved her brother, she was glad to get his approval.

"You ain't surprised at all?"

"No, we knew it would happen. We didn't know how long it would take him to get the nerve to ask. Well, have you set a date?"

"Soon, maybe in a couple months."

"Well, I guess we need to get you a house built. It's for shore that one ain't gone hold all of us."

"Yeah, that is for sure."

Rob and Ben took the two big wagons and headed for Dallas. It was a long trip, about two weeks, round trip. But it was the closest place to buy enough lumber to build a house. On the way back, they stopped at Alto's store. The door was locked. A sheet of paper was folded over an envelope and tacked to the door. Rob pulled the paper from the door and read it.

"Well, what does it say?" asked Ben.

"Mr Alto is dead. This store will be closed till the new owner takes over."

"Damn, Mr. Alto died?" said Ben. "I wonder what happened to him. The last time we saw him, about two weeks ago, he was fine."

"The envelope is addressed to Jennie Baker." Rob said. "I wonder what this is all about."

"I think you should open it?"

"No, " said Rob, "I think I will let her open it."

They found his grave, under some oaks about fifty yards from the store. "I used to see him sitting here under these trees. Guess he liked this spot," said Ben.

They pitched camp next to the store. Ben stopped the wagon in front of the house. It was a happy reunion. Ben and Rob had been gone over a month. Rob took the papers from his pocket, and handed them to Jennie.

"Here, this was tacked to the door of Mr. Alto's store."

She read the papers. Jennie put her hand over her mouth. "I can't believe this," she said.

"Looks like you own yourself a store, and 5000 acres of land to go with it," said Rob.

"Why me?" she asked.

Rob just shook his head. Ben pulled another small, neatly folded piece of paper from the envelop. He unfolded it and read it.

"Here read this, it might answer some of your questions," said Ben. Jennie read it out loud.

"I think you are a remarkable woman, and you are an all-around good person. I never got a chance to know my daughter. Her mother took her from me when she was four years old. I would like to think she grew up to be just like you. I can't give anything to her, so I leave it to you. Her name was Carliene Marie Alto."

Jennie folded the papers and put them back into the envelope. "I'll deal with this later. Right now I got a wedding to plan." She walked away with tears in her eyes. Rob watched her walk away. "Well Ben, I guess we will deal with that later." Ben nodded, with a grin he said, "I guess so."

They decided to build the house across the yard, in front of the main house, under a big oak tree. Carlos and Jaun took charge of the house building. "I am not the best carpenter, but I think me and Jaun can get it done."

Everybody pitched in when they could, and when they had time. It took them three weeks to finish it. There was enough lumber for a small back porch, and a front porch.

"Well, there you go Jennie. Got you a brand new house," said Annie.

"Yep, now all I got to do is get married."

Rob exploded into laughter. Ben stood there with a lost look on his face. Jennie laughed too. She put her arms around him. Ben broke out in a big grin.

"When we have kids we can add on," said Jennie.

Al and Patty brought their son Jake, and Mr. Nelson to the wedding. They came two days early.

"I don't want to miss any of this," said Al.

"Me neither," said Patty.

Carlos and Jaun cooked a pig on the pit. It was a labor of love for Carlos. He liked to cook. Jaun didn't like it too much, but he liked helping his father. There wasn't a preacher close by. With the help of Rob, they would say their vows. Rob stood on the top step, Ben and Jennie stood on the bottom.

"Are we ready?" asked Rob. Jennie and Ben nodded.

"Jennie, do you wish to marry this man, Ben Adams?"

"I do."

"Do you take him for who he is, to stick with him through thick or thin?"

"I do."

"Ben, do you wish to marry this woman, Jennie Baker?"

"I do."

"You promise to protect her and be a good husband?"

"I do."

"Well I say here in front of God, family and friends as witnesses, that you are man and wife."

Rob stepped down in front of the couple. He joined their hands. "Welcome to the family brother."

"Thanks, I hope I can be a good husband and brother in law to all of you."

"You will."

"Jennie, I think you got a good man here, treat him well."

"I plan to."

"There is only one thing left to do," said Mr. Nelson. "We get to kiss the bride."

"That's right," said Ben. "After me."

He took Jennie in his arms and gave her a big kiss. Everybody clapped their hands. There was plenty of well wishes and hugs from everybody. Carlos rang his bell. "If everybody is ready, so is the pig."

During the first few months of her marriage, Jennie grew closer to Ben. She found out that he was stronger and tougher than she thought. When she told him about the money she and Rob buried, he smiled.

"You are something, and smarter than most of the men in this state."

"I know that you and Rob have worked hard to build this ranch. I also know that you are the thread that holds it together. I'll will help ya'll run this ranch."

That told Jennie a lot about the man she married. She loved him all the more for it. "I think I got me a real man," she thought.

CHAPTER 14

It has been a year since the war ended. Times were hard here in Texas. Most people were just working to eat. Texas, like the rest of the south, was broke.

The hide man came and bought a few cows. Jennie sold fifty head to the Union army. It was a onetime deal. They packed up and moved out after a couple of months. Jennie rode her horse to the barn. She unsaddled him and turned him out into the corral.

When she started across the yard, she saw a man riding up on a mule. He saw Jennie and rode over to her and dismounted. Jennie always carried a pistol. She unfastened the strap that held it in the holster.

"Can I help you?" she asked.

"I am Mason. Me and my brothers were here several months ago." Jennie looked at him. "Yes I remember you, and your brothers." She shook hands then invited him to join her on the front porch.

"Well, what brings you back our way?"

He pointed to the road. There was a wagon parked at the end of the drive. Jennie could see that his family and their belongings were on the wagon.

"Care to tell me what happened to your ranch?"

"Lost it. Our paw died shortly after we got home. Ain't no money to be made. When them damn yankee carpetbaggers came, they said we owed them two hundred dollars, or get off the land. So we left."

Jennie leaned back in her chair. "These are some hard times we goin' through alright."

"We was hoping maybe you would allow us to camp down there next to the creek for a few days and rest up."

"Sure," said Jennie.

Mason looked at his mule. "I know she ain't much, but I will trade her for some flower and lard. We ain't eat much the last few days." Mason hung his head, and with his hat in his hands. "I guess this is the same as begging. And I am. Not for me," he turned his head toward the wagon, "for them I will."

"You don't have to beg Mason, we will be glad to help," she said. She went into the house, and walked into the kitchen. Maria was taking some bread from the oven. Jennie stood there, thinking.

"Is something wrong?" Maria asked.

"Do you remember the three soldiers that came here right after the war?"

"Yes I do."

"They are back, they lost their ranch."

"Now you are wondering if we got enough food cooked, to feed them too."

Jennie grinned, and nodded. "I think we do."

"No, I got another idea. Karla, get some corn meal, some lard and dry beans sacked up when I get back."

Jennie joined Mason, "Go get your folks. Bring them up here. See that tall tree behind the barn?"

"Yes ma'am."

"Park your wagon there and pitch camp."

"Are you sure about that?"

"Mason, you just do what I say."

"Go, go get um up here."

Mason put his hat back on and rode his mule back to the wagon. "Follow me, these folks are nice enough to let us camp here tonight."

Rex stopped the wagon under the big tree. "This is a good spot to make camp alright," he said.

"Yeah," said Mason, "let's get this place ready, so we can get a good night's sleep."

"We won't have to sleep with one eye open," said Rex.

Their mother, Ruth, looked at the barns, the houses, the corral. "This is the kind of place your paw had in mind. If it weren't for that war."

"Maw, we said we wasn't gone talk about the past," said Lewis.

Jennie and Ben came up on a buck board. They all got acquainted. "I brought you some groceries. There's a smoked pork shoulder, some beans, corn meal and lard."

"Lordy, Miss Jennie, that's a lot of food," said Mason.

"And you are more than welcome to it."

Ruth started to cry. She sat down in her rocking chair, one of the few things she was able to bring with her. Lisa stood beside her and put her arm around her shoulder.

"Losing that house and land is hard on mama."

"I can only imagine how I would feel," said Jennie.

"We will be out of your way in the morning, so if we are gone before you all are up and out, we thank ya, all of you."

"No, no," said Ben, "you folks can stay right here for a few days. Them mules need the rest. And I think Miss Ruth needs a rest too."

"That's settled, you folks just take it easy. I'll be back," said Jennie.

Jennie managed to keep them around for a week. At supper that night, Jennie asked everybody what they thought of the Pitts family. They all agreed.

"They are some nice folks," said Annie.

"I want to ask the Pitts family to stay. We need some help around here. I think they will fit in here just fine."

Rob spoke first. "As for me, I agree. We do need the help. We know these folks."

"Okay by me," said Ben.

"Then we all agree?"

"I think you should be the one to ask," said Ben.

"We will all ask 'um," said Rob.

It didn't take much to talk the Pitts family into staying. "You will have to camp under the tree for a while longer," Rob said.

"That will be ok." Said Ruth. "Just staying in one place will be a blessing to us."

Rob brought some tarps. They built two rooms so they could have some privacy. "This will be just fine," said Ruth.

CHAPTER 15

During the next few months with the extra help, they branded a lot of cows. They had over a hundred head of bulls and older cows separated from the rest. When the hide man came, he paid fifty cents a head.

"Ain't much, but every little bit counts," said Jennie.

The hide man gave them some good news. The railroad was in Abilene Kansas.

"They will buy every cow you bring."

"That's a long way from here," said Jennie.

"Some ranchers are drivin' herds from San Antonio."

"Where is Abilene?" asked Rob.

"From here, head north west. You will cut a trail left by the other herds. Just follow it right into Abilene."

"I know that country pretty good," said Ben. That was the conversation for a few days on the Baker ranch.

"I say we round up as many cows as we can and drive them north," Ben said.

"I don't think it will be that easy," said Jennie.

"I know, but we can do it."

"Jaun, how many steers can we get together in the next three or four days?"

"I think maybe 400, maybe 500 head."

"At four or five dollars a head, that will be a lot of money," said Jaun.

"I think we need to get started," said Ben.

The next morning, Jennie took Annie and her son, Noah Martin and left for the Nelson ranch. Jennie told Al the plan.

"How many steers can you gather in the next week?"

Al thought a minute. "I don't think I will be able to get a herd together on such short notice."

"It is short notice alright," said Jennie.

"We sold most of our older cows to the hide man. Money wise, we are doing fine."

"Well, if there is a next year, we'll be more prepared, "said Jennie.

"I owe you some money off that hide deal," Al said.

"No, you keep it."

"That wasn't our deal."

"Don't worry about that damn deal. We are family. That's the deal."

Jennie and Annie left the next morning. They will be needed at home, getting ready to take the cows to Abilene. They managed to gather over five hundred cows that would be beef cows.

"We got them in one location," said Jaun, "but we can't keep them there long."

Carlos worked on the two wagons, getting them ready to make the long trip.

"Are them wagons ready?" Ben asked.

"I think so."

"Good," said Ben. "We need to get going."

"Are we ready?" asked Jennie.

"I don't think we will ever be ready," said Ben, "but we are going to leave the day after tomorrow."

Jennie overheard Ben talking to Rob about who would be going on the drive.

"Me, Jaun, Mason, Rex, Lewis, and maybe Manny. He can drive one the wagons."

"And me," said Jennie, "I can drive the other wagon."

"Now look here, this ain't gonna be no Sunday drive," said Ben.

"No need to argue, I am going."

Ben stared at his wife for a minute, then with a disgusted look on his face.

"Alright, but on this drive, I will be the boss. Is that clear?"

"Clear. You will be the boss."

She didn't like going against her husband, but this time she was right. Everything was ready. The cows were gathered on the west side of the ranch, about five miles from the house. They planned to leave at first light.

They had just finished supper; Annie went to her bedroom. She heard a knock at the door. When she opened it, she was surprised to see her brother, "Al, what in the world are you doing here? Well, don't stand there come on in."

"Look who's here."

They were even more surprised when they found out why he was there. "I decided to go with ya'll. I know you will be shorthanded. I just felt like I was needed, so here I am."

Jennie poured Rob some more coffee. 'What about Patty?" said Annie.

"I tried to get the three of them to come here and stay, but they wanted to stay and take care of the ranch."

Rob told Al that he and Annie would pay them a visit later, to make sure everything was alright. Ben got to his feet, "Well, guess I will head out to the herd."

"I will go with you," Al said.

They pointed the herd west. Denton Texas was a hundred miles. That would be the first real town on the map. From there they would turn north. After the first few days, they realized how hard this trip would be. It took several days for them to get used to sitting in the saddle for hours at a time. They got supplies at Denton. Two days later, they picked up the trail made by previous drives. Ben and Mason sat in their saddles, looking at the tracks.

"Ain't gonna be hard to follow that trail," said Mason.

"Nope, when the herd gets here, all we gotta do is follow these tracks north."

And that's what they did, day after day it was the same, eat, sleep, ride. It was an uneventful trip. No Indians, no rustlers, no stampedes. Ben was glad things were going smooth.

He felt sorry for Jennie, but there was nothing he could do to make it easier for her. She was tough alright, he doubted there was another woman that could hold up through this. He knew there were days when she had female trouble. He tried to help, the rest of the boys too. Manny tried to pick up the slack, but Jennie would have none of that. She earned the respect of them all.

"I say one thing Ben," said Mason, "that's one hell of a woman you got there."

The days turned into weeks, they would lose track of time. Only when they would meet somebody on the trail, or go into a town for supplies did they catch up on their location and the date. These last two weeks, they hadn't seen anybody. Ben was getting worried. He may have to send Mason to look for a store. They were getting low on food. Jaun came riding at him fast. He reined his horse in and stopped alongside Ben.

"Hold on there boy, what the hell?"

"Miss Jennie said for you to come."

"Is she hurt?"

"No, she ain't hurt, there's two men talkin' to her. They are from Abilene."

"Yee ha," yelled Ben, "let's go."

Jennie was in the buggy with two men. They sat watching the cows go by. Ben and Jaun stopped and dismounted. Jennie introduced everybody. "Mr. Isaac and Mr. Thornton are from the cattle company. They are here to buy our cows." Jennie was so excited she was almost out of breath. "They are from Abilene."

"So we made it," said Ben." Jennie had a big grin on her face, she nodded her head real fast.

"How far is it to town?" asked Ben.

"About three miles," said Isaac. "As a matter of fact, when you get the point of your herd over that rise you need to stop."

"Jaun, go tell the boys."

"Those aren't long horns; what breed are they?" asked Mr. Thornton.

"I don't know," said Jennie. "My paw brought them here from Alabama. I don't think they were any one breed. He always bought cows from people, so they were mixed. We have crossed them with long horns."

"They are better looking cows than what we have seen so far," said Mr. Isaac. "How many head you got?"

"We started with a little over five hundred, we lost a few, so it will be hard to give you an exact number," said Ben.

"Don't need it," said Thornton. "Just wanting an estimate. We will count them."

"We will buy the herd from you," said Isaac.

"That's why we are here," said Jennie.

Isaac and Thornton walked away from the buggy, they talked, then came back. "We pay 12 dollars a head for longhorns, but for these cows you got more meat on them. We'll pay seventeen," said Isaac.

Jennie sat on the buggy with her mouth wide open. Ben didn't say anything, just stood looking at the two men. He turned his head and looked at Jennie. She stared back at him.

"Did I hear you say 17 dollars?" asked Ben.

"You did, when we get them loaded onto the train cars, we will get a final tally, and you will get your money," said Isaac, "do we have a deal?"

"Yes sir," said Jennie, "you got a deal."

"Good, we will see you in town."

"In the meantime, just hold them out here, I will send for them tomorrow. My men will take over," said Isaac.

"Yes sir, whatever you say," said Jennie.

They signed the agreement, then the two men left. She watched them ride away. She turned to look at Ben, "Seventeen dollars Ben, did ya hear, seventeen dollars." She took off her hat and tossed it into the air, then let out shrill "yeee haaa!" She jumped at Ben. He grabbed her around the waist. With her feet dangling off the ground, she gave him a big kiss. Al and Mason rode up in a cloud of dust. Still dangling in Ben's arms, she looked at them.

"We made it boys, we made it," she said. "We made it."

They all decided to stay with the herd that night. The next morning, some men came and took over. They got the herd headed towards the loading pens. Jennie, Ben, and Al sat on the top rail of the loading pen.

"As soon as we get paid for these cows," Jennie said, "I will get us a room over at that fancy hotel. Take me a long hot bath, then sleep for two days."

"That sounds like a winner to me," said Al. The tally man wrote the numbers on a piece of paper, and he gave it to a young man.

"Follow him, you'll get paid." They followed him over to Mr. Isaac's office.

"Come in, have a seat." They sat around his desk. Jennie sat on the edge of her chair, in anticipation. Mr. Isaac was busy. Figuring up the tally.

"Well folks, I think this will be the price."

Jennie looked at the paper. Four hundred ninety-two at 17.00 dollars, equals eight thousand three hundred and sixty-four dollars.

"You want it in cash or a check?"

"I think we will take cash," said Ben. "Can we get a thousand now, and rest when we leave?"

"Sure, just let me know, and I will have it ready for ya." Ben took the thousand dollars from Mr. Isaac.

"I hope you bring more cows next year," said Mr. Isaac.

"If all goes well, we hope to double that number," said Jennie.

Ben stopped at the door, "Here Jennie, I recon this money is yours."

"No, you keep it, and it is our money. It will be safer with you." She reached over and pulled out a hundred-dollar bill.

"I will take this off your hands," she said with a grin. Then walked toward the hotel.

"If you want me, I'll be in my room. Taking a bath. After I buy me some new clothes." He gave each of them a hundred dollars.

"That orta be enough money to spend here in town. We can settle up when we get back to the ranch."

"A hundred dollars," said Mason. "I ain't had this much money at one time in my life."

"Hells fire, I ain't seen this much money before," said Rob.

"You boys try to stay out of trouble," said Ben.

"We wouldn't be standing here admiring this money, if it wasn't for you fellas," said Ben.

CHAPTER 16

Abilene was a young town. The big herds from Texas were just starting to make their way here. It would get bigger and wilder as time passed. There was only one hotel, a saloon, barber shop, restaurant and two general merchandise stores. All on the west side of the railroad tracks, all the residents of Abilene worked and lived there.

The cowboys stayed mostly on the other side of the tracks. It was made up of saloons, gambling houses, cheap hotels, and whore's houses. There was a constant sound of hammers driving nails. By the next year, Abilene would triple in size and population. Today, there might be a hundred or so cowboys here, next year that number will grow.

Ben went to the store and bought him some new clothes, then went to the barber shop. The sign read, 'hot bath, shave, haircut, one dollar'.

"Boy, these folks got the prices jacked up. They are trying to get some of that cattle money." When he left the barber shop, he went to the hotel. The clerk told him which room Jennie was in. He knocked on the door. "It's me Ben."

"You got a key?"

"Yeah."

"Come in."

"You're still in the tub, I bet you're soaked all the hot out of that water."

"I was almost asleep when you knocked on the door." She stood up, and got out of the tub. Ben stared at her naked body.

"Damn," he thought, "I almost forgot what a sexy woman she is."

She dried off, then fell back on the bed laying on her back with her arms stretched out and her legs spread apart. It was almost more than Ben could take. He took off his clothes and got into the tub of water. He took a quick bath. Ben stood by the tub drying off. He heard a noise coming from the main room. He stuck his head around the corner. Jennie was lying there snoring.

"Damn the bad luck," he said. She turned over on her side, Ben lay down beside her and fell asleep. When he woke up, he was lying on his stomach. Jennie snuggled against him with her arm over his shoulders and her leg on his butt. He wanted to wake her, but if anybody needed this rest, she did. So, he tried not to move. After a few minutes she spoke into his ear, "I am awake."

For the next hour, they caught up on their love making. Exhausted, they both lay on the bed. Jennie was cuddled in his arms. They both fell asleep again. Jennie woke Ben. "We better get dressed. I am hungry."

"You had enough rest?"

"I have had enough of everything for now. After I eat and get my strength back, I will need some more," she paused, "everything."

"Hot damn, let's go eat." He grabbed her around her waist and swung her around. "I love you girl."

"And I love you too." She gave him a big kiss. "Now let's get a move on."

They got dressed and went down stairs. They found Al sitting on the porch of the hotel in a rocking chair.

"Well finally, I was about to send somebody up there to see if ya'll was alive."

"We are," said Jennie, "and I am starving." Al got to his feet. "Let's eat."

The rest of the crew spent their time across the tracks. Taking advantage of the saloons and the abundance of women. At a price of course.

The next day they all went shopping. Buying things, they have been doing without for the last few years. Ben sold one of the wagons and most of the horses, and everything else they didn't need to get home. He wanted to travel light.

"Tell the boys, we will be pulling out tomorrow."

Al grinned, "I hope they are able."

"Me too."

Another herd arrived, which meant more cowboys. Ben, Jennie and Al, sat on the porch of the hotel. They could hear the pianos and the laughter, mostly the shrills of the saloon girls, across the tracks. They sat there on the porch drinking whiskey and smoking cigars. They talked about what they would do once they got back to the ranch.

"Ya'll got some big plans," Jennie said, "1 hope we can do half what you talking about."

"It ain't out of the question, Jennie girl," said Al.

"With that, I will go to my room and get some sleep." She looked at Ben, "are you coming?"

He stood up, "Yep. It will be a while before we sleep in a bed again." They got in the bed, but they didn't go to sleep. The sun was just coming up. Ben and Jennie were getting their things packed. A knock came at the door. It was Al.

"Ben, the marshal is down stairs, he wants to see you."

"Did he say why?"

"Nope. You go find out what he wants," said Al. "I will help Jennie."

Ben walked out onto the porch. He grinned, "Well, Marshal Smith, been awhile."

Ben met Marshall Smith several years ago. He was tough as they come, and honest. "Howdy Ben, I didn't have no idea it was you I was lookin' for. Last I heard, you was still a Texas Ranger."

"I done got married, working at a ranch east of Dallas."

"Well, I be dog gone. Glad for ya."

"Thanks. What business we got this early in the morning?"

"Seems like one of your hands done got hisself in a peck of trouble. Name is Lewis."

"Yeah, he works for me, what the hell kinda trouble is he in? He ain't no trouble maker. Good boy."

"He beat the shit out of Lester Garfield last night. Lester is looking for him. Aims to get even. By even I mean, kill him. Ben, this Lester fella is good with a gun, and he doesn't mind using it. When I heard Lewis was over here on this side of the tracks, well I can't have no shootin' and killin' goin' on."

"Why don't you arrest this Garfield fella. Hold him till we get out of town?"

"You know I cain't do that. He ain't done nothing wrong. If ya'll can leave town before he finds Lewis, well that would solve everything."

"We plan to leave, soon as I get them up."

"Good, that takes a load off me Ben, and thanks." A man joined them. "Marshal, Lester knows that young fella is here."

"Damn," said the marshal. "You folks get a move I will try to hold him off." Ben went upstairs. "Al, get everybody loaded up, and headed out of town. Rob, you go to Mr. Isaac's office. He will be there with our money. I will catch up with you."

"What's going on?" asked Al.

"Just do what I say. We can talk later. Let me borrow that pistol."

Ben had his gun belt on, he carried one pistol here in town. He put Al's gun in the belt. He stepped out into the hall. He checked the pistols to make sure they were loaded. Rex came running down the hall. "Where you goin'?" asked Ben. Rex was wide eyed. "There is a man outside. He has a gun. He is looking for Lewis."

Ben took Rex by the front of his shirt, "Calm down boy."

"I gotta warn Lewis."

"No, I will take care of this. You stay here, do not, I repeat, do not let Lewis come down those stars. Do you hear me?"

"Yes sir."

Ben went down stairs. He stopped at the front door of the hotel. He looked outside. He could see Garfield standing in the middle of the street. He had a pistol in each hand. Garfield had been drinking, trying to get up enough courage to kill Lewis.

"Come out here you asshole, let's see how brave you are."

Ben took a deep breath then exhaled. He opened the door and walked outside. He stood there looking at Garfield.

"What the hell do you want?" asked Garfield.

"You lookin' for Lewis?"

"That's right, and you ain't him."

"You gotta go through me, or take your ass whipping like a man, and get back across them railroad tracks."

"I didn't come here lookin' for you, I came lookin' for Lewis. Now get him out here."

"You play with me."

With that, Lester cocked his pistol and pointed it at Ben and fired. The bullet hit the steps in front of Ben. Ben fired back. The bullet hit Lester in his left arm. The force of the bullet knocked his arm back. His pistol went flying from his hand. Lester raised the other pistol and fired a second time. The bullet went into the dirt.

Ben steadied his gun and fired back. This time he hit Lester in his chest. Lester dropped his pistol and grabbed his shirt. He fell to his knees. Pink blood came from his mouth, he fell forward, dead. Ben walked over and looked down at Lester satisfied, he was dead. He went outside. The marshal walked up with a shotgun. He smiled at Ben.

"Boy, I am glad it is you. What if it had the other fella?"

"I guess we'll never know now, will we?"

"Do me a favor. Make sure folks know it was me that killed Lester. Lewis doesn't need this hanging around his neck. I'll do it."

"Well, if I ain't under arrest, I will catch up with them wagons, we got a long ride ahead of us." Marshall Smith lowered the shotgun. "Have a safe journey."

"Thanks," said Ben. He looked at the marshal and nodded.

CHAPTER 17

Ben caught up with them about a mile outside of town. He didn't join them right away. He rode behind the wagons for a while. After supper that night, he told them what happened. When he stopped talking, he told them that he didn't want to talk about it again.

"You know what and why. That's enough." Lewis met with his brothers a few yards from the wagons.

"I can't believe he didn't tell us."

"Yeah, he laid his life on the line, alright," said Rex.

"He had more than just his life on the line," said Mason, "he laid everything he has and everything he will ever have on the line. All for us." Said Lewis.

"If that man killed you, me and Rex would have gone after him. Chances are one of us, maybe both of us, might have got killed. Don't you boys forget that. Cause I shore won't, ever."

"I wish I could tell him how I feel about all this," said Lewis.

"He knows, just let it be boys, just let it be," said Mason.

The day before they got to the ranch, Ben sent Jaun on ahead.

"Tell your mama, she better have supper ready when I get there. I am more than ready for some of her cookin'."

"You bet I will."

It was late when Jennie stopped the wagon in front of the house. Nothing ever looked so good. Maria and Annie had them a feast cooked. Ben pushed his plate back. "I am full as a tick on a fat dog."

All through supper, Jennie could sense something was wrong. She was too tired to worry about tonight. She would find out in the morning. For now, she was going home and get into her own bed. Rob and Annie came over just after daylight. Jennie poured them some coffee, then sat down across from them.

"Ok, somebody talk, what's going on here?" Annie sat across from Jennie. She reached over and took Jennie's hand. "It's bad, really bad."

Rob took a deep breath, "Patty is dead, so is little Jake and Mr. Nelson." Jennie and Ben sat in unbelief. Ben shook his head like he was trying to wake from a dream.

"Say that again."

"It's true, Ben." said Annie.

Tears ran down Jennie's face. "No, I just can't believe it." She laid her head on the table and cried. Ben put his hand on her shoulder. He looked at Rob. "How, I mean what happened?"

"Three weeks after ya'll left, I took Annie and Noah to visit. We planned to stay a few days. When we got there, they were all dead. We found Mr. Nelson out by the chicken pen. He had been shot in the back. His pistol was still in his holster. They must have sneaked up on him. Jake was out back, they shot him too. It looked like they drag him back there." Rob stopped talking.

"What about Patty?" asked Ben.

"She was in the bedroom." Jennie threw up her hands. "No more, I don't want to hear any more."

"Good," said Rob, "I don't want to tell you either."

"Al, does he know?" asked Ben. Rob nodded. "We told him this morning. He never said a word. He saddled his horse and left."

"We need to go to him," said Jennie. "He shouldn't be there by himself."

"No, I think maybe we will go first thing in the morning," said Rob. "I would want to be by myself, if it was me."

"Maybe you are right," said Ben. "We will leave first thing in the morning."

"Poor Patty." said Jennie.

"Poor Al, he's got to live with it," said Annie.

Rob, Annie, Ben and Jennie arrived at the Nelson ranch late the next day. Al was sitting on the porch. He had his pistol and a jug of whiskey on the table in front of him. Annie knelt down beside him. He looked at his sister, "This is hard Annie."

"I know."

"Why, I keep asking, but there ain't no answer."

"They cleaned out the smoke house, took most of the chickens, and the horses, and the wagon. Why did they have to kill 'um? Just take the stuff and go."

It was awkward, nobody knew what to say. Al sat on the porch all night. Just after daylight, Ben heard a gunshot, he grabbed his pistol and ran out onto the porch. Al was lying on the floor beside the table. He had blown one side of his head off. Ben grabbed the blanket from Al's lap and covered his head, before Jennie and Annie came out.

Rob joined Ben on the porch, "Is he dead?"

"Yep."

"Damn, now them girls got to deal with this," said Rob.

Al wrote two letters. The killers never found Mr. Nelson's money. Al put it all in a sack and placed it under the steps. With trembling hands, Annie read the letter out loud.

"Annie, I hate to end it this way, it ain't fair to you. I just can't live with it. I should have stayed here. Maybe they would still be alive. Don't feel sad for me. I am better off, I ain't suffering no more.

I leave all the money to Annie. I leave everything else to Noah Martin. Look under the steps for the money. The deed is in the other envelope. You have been a good sister. The rest of you were a good family. Couldn't' ask for no better."

Al Nelson.

They buried him next to his wife and son. Rob walked Annie back to the house, she could hardly stand. Jennie stood at the foot of Patty's grave. "This is such a shame. She was a good girl. I loved her so much." Jennie burst out in tears. Ben held on to her and led her to the porch.

"What do you want to do with this house?" asked Rob.

"Lock it up," said Annie.

Rob held the sack of money. Annie looked at it, then at Rob. She shook her head slowly from side to side. She tried to speak, but nothing came out.

"When we get home, I will put it away somewhere. When Noah Martin gets old enough, it will be his present from the Nelson family.

She nodded, "Good, that will be good."

CHAPTER 18

It will take Jennie and Rob a long time to get over the death of their sister Patty. The death of Al affected Annie the most. The fact that he killed himself was hard for her to accept. But with the passing of each day she got better even though they went back to their chores, and it was good therapy, there was a dark cloud over them all. It was going to be a long time for this to heal.

Jennie spent most of her time at the main house. She watched Noah Martin. Annie wasn't herself. Maria or Karla kept Annie in sight at all times. Jennie sat in a rocking chair on the front porch. She took Noah Martin and let him in the yard. She sat thinking.

After a few days, she asked Ben to invite Rob and Annie to their house. Jennie figured they would have more privacy there. They all sat around the kitchen table. With the death of the Nelson family, nobody thought about the success of the cattle drive. When Jennie placed the money on the table, Rob looked at her, "Damn Jennie, I plum forgot about this."

"We all did," said Ben.

"We got a ranch to run here, and people that work here," said Jennie.

"I have had a few days here to do some thinking. I got some ideas about the future. If ya'll got a better idea, by all means say so. First, I want to give everybody that works on this ranch a hundred dollars. We'll keep a couple of hundred for our own personal use. The rest will be used to run the ranch. With what we already had added to the money we got from the drive, we will have about seven thousand dollars in cash."

"I never dreamed we would have that much money," said Rob, "never."

"Now you know, since the war, all them scallywags, outlaws, lowlifes, just scum of the earth. They are all comin' to Texas."

Rob spoke up, "I talked to one of them trail bosses back in Abilene. He works on a ranch south of here. He told me we were lucky. They are having trouble with horse thieves and cattle rustlers," said Ben.

"We are going to buy some barbed wire," said Jennie.

"Barbed wire?"

"There's one more thing, I think we need to reopen Mr. Alto's store. The store will belong to the four of us, not just me." They sat pondering what she had said.

Rob put both hands on the table. "I agree. How 'bout you?" He asked looking at Annie. "Sounds good to me, but I have one question, who is going to run that store?"

"Yeah, damn good question too," said Ben.

"Well, there's Ben, Rob, Mason, and Carlos." Jennie said.

"I can tell you right now, count me out," said Ben.

"Me too, I ain't sittin' in no store all day," said Rob, "No, no." With that, Ben and Rob walked out on the front porch.

"She is crazy if she thinks I am going for that idea," said Rob.

"It is her idea to open the store, " said Ben. "She can run it."

Rob grinned, "She does a pretty good job of running everything else. I reckon she'll do a pretty damn good job of that to."

Jennie put most of time into opening the store. Karla and Lisa were a big help. The three of them put in a lot of hours. Jennie needed somebody to run this store. She advertised for a store keeper. She received several letters. She settled on one couple. Edgar Honeycutt and his wife, Jane. Mr. Honeycutt was a short man, about 5 feet 3 inches. His wife was taller by two inches. She was a slim woman, with jet black hair and black eyes.

"Miss Adams, before you give us this job, there's something you should know. Jane's mother was a slave. Her father was a Choctaw Indian. Without going into a lot of details, we were married about twelve years ago. We were forced to leave our home. We have been working our way west ever since. Now, here we are in Texas. If that will be a problem, we can leave now and save us both a lot of trouble."

"Well, if I am any judge of people, she must be a very good person or you would not be married to her."

"I think the two of you will do a good job running this store for us," Jennie reached out her hand, "shake on it?" With a smile and a look of relief on his face, they shook hands.

Jennie sent for a salesman. She let Edgar do the order. He knew more about what they needed to stock the shelves. Edgar and Jane stood outside the store. Jennie, Ben, Rob, Annie, Lisa and Karla were there; it was the grand opening.

"Well," said Ben, "you girls did it, you got a store, ready for customers. I think I will be the first one." With that, Jennie turned to Edgar and Jane, "There it is."

Later, Jennie met with Edgar, "I just want you to know a few things. My family makes our money raising cattle. No matter if this store makes money or not, you will get paid. If anybody, neighbor or stranger comes here and needs help, we help them. If they can't pay, it will get paid. The other thing is, we don't cheat people, we give them a good product at a fair price."

"I believe you, it's refreshing to hear you say that. Most owners believe the opposite."

Jennie called a family meeting. As usual, they met at her house. "Well, what are we gonna discuss?" asked Annie with a grin.

Jennie served everybody coffee. Then sat down beside Annie. "Discuss is right, and I hope we can all agree on this."

"Well, let's hear it," said Ben.

"I think we should make Mason our range foreman. Put him in charge of the cattle."

"I don't have a problem with that," said Rob.

"Me either," said Ben, "he knows more about cows than I will ever know, and I don't mind saying it."

"The funny thing is, I had the same thoughts myself. Watching him work, you just know, there's a cowboy."

"We all look to him for advice every day," said Jennie.

"Well, how much are you gonna pay him?" asked Annie.

"What do you think we should pay him?" asked Jennie.

"You pay everybody else 30 dollars a month, he will have twice the responsibility, I'd say 60 dollars orta do it. With a bonus after the drive to Abilene, a good bonus."

"Damn, who's side are you on?" asked Ben. That got a laugh from everyone.

"I agree," said Jennie. "Anybody oppose?"

"No," said Rob.

"Good, we got that settled," said Jennie. "Now the next thing, we need lumber to build houses and barns, a bigger corral. We need to build the Pitts family a house. Carlos and Maria need a better house. I talked to the lumber salesman. He can deliver what we need, plus the carpenters to build it."

"At what cost?" asked Rob.

"We can't get an exact figure, but a rough estimate, about five hundred dollars, maybe six, at the most."

"This is something we need, and we got the money, I say we get started on this as soon as possible," said Rob.

"Do you all agree?" asked Jennie.

"Yep, all agree," said Ben. "And I say Rob orta look after all this building."

"I agree," said Annie.

Jennie laughed out loud. "Hell yeah."

Rob looked at his wife, "Thanks honey."

"Annie, the next thing I want do is, and this is up to you. I would like to buy some of them longhorns and put them on the Nelson land. We will split the profit fifty fifty." Annie was looking down at the table. She raised her head and looked at Rob, "I don't have no objections to that. Makes sense to me. What do you say?"

"I say Noah Martin will be rich by the time he gets grown."

"Good said, Ben. We can go to the Smith ranch west of here, I am sure he will sell us some of his longhorns. I will take care of that."

"Thanks Annie." Jennie said then stood up, "I took the liberty of asking Mason to join us here."

"I think he just rode up," said Rob.

She went to the front door and motioned him to come into the house. "Ben, he will be working with you on a daily basis, so I think you should tell him the news." After Ben told him, Jennie asked the question, "do you and your family plan to stay? And do you want this responsibility?"

Mason stood at the end of the table with his hat in his hand. "Yes ma'am, we all kinda look at this ranch as home. Yes ma'am, we will be here till you run us off."

"Well hell, that ain't gone happen," said Ben.

"Glad that this is settled, now let's all get busy building the biggest ranch in Texas," said Jennie.

The Pitts family were more than glad to get a house. Maria was proud of her new home. Rob built two new barns. One was a mile from the ranch house. It would be used for hay, if and when they could get that much hay. Jennie and Rob sat in the buckboard, looking at the new buildings.

"Rob, I think Uncle Noah saw all this in his mind from the first day we decided to settle here. I don't think he would be surprised if he came back."

"I will admit; I didn't see this happening."

"Me neither."

One of the first things Mason did was to divide the ranch up into 4 sections north, south, east, and west. Then he numbered the pastures. Now everybody knew where to go. Ben, Mason and Rex went to the Smith ranch to buy longhorns.

"Ben, I don't think you need to buy one of them longhorn bulls. The last time I was on the Nelson ranch, I saw a couple of nice bulls. We just need some cows."

"If that's what you want to do, then that's what we will do."

"I think we will get a good mix breed to sell."

"Sounds like a damn good idea to me."

When they got the cows back, Ben told Jennie and Rob what Mason suggested. They both thought it was a good idea. Jennie and Ben sat under the shade tree. They were waiting for Mason to join them.

"There he comes," said Ben. Mason rode up and dismounted. "Am I late?"

"No not at all," Jennie answered.

Mason took off his hat, "Well, I know you are wondering why I wanted to meet with the two of you."

"Yeah, we was kinda wondering about that," said Ben.

"We got some big hay barns, that is a good idea about hay. If they was full, we could feed the cows all winter. They wouldn't lose so much weight. More of them would survive the winter."

"What are you trying to say here Mason? That we need the barns full of hay?"

"We don't have time to cut that much hay. It will take us all summer to fill them barns with hay."

"You are right Mason. Me and Ben have been talking about that very thing. It will take time, but we have a plan to get those barns full and keep them full. In the meantime, we will cut what we can."

Jennie advertised for farmers. To her surprise, four farmers and their families showed up at the store. Mr. Alto left her 5000 acres. 350 of those acres, were across the creek. She told them she would give each of them 80 acres to work, if they agreed to raise hay and corn. "I will buy your crops at a fair market price. I will provide lumber for houses, barns and corrals. If you stay 5 years, I will give you the land. Well, what do ya say?" They all agreed.

Rob and Ben were amazed at Jennie's ability to run the business end of the ranch, and how she made it all happen. They had an addition built onto Jennie's house, "We need an office, this is the best place for it."

CHAPTER 19

After supper, Jennie and Ben sat on their front porch. Two men came riding up into the yard.

"Howdy folks."

"Howdy," said Ben, "what can we do for ya?"

"We lookin' for the Pitts family, they are kin. We understand they work hereabouts."

"They do," said Ben. "Follow me, I'll take you to the house."

After Ben was satisfied that everything was alright, he went back home. Thirty minutes later, he saw Mason coming. The two young men were with him. They stayed on their horses, Mason joined them on the porch.

"These two boys are cousins. They just came from Mississippi. Well, they lookin' for work."

It was still light enough for Jennie to see. The two boys were about 20 years old. Their clothes were ragged, and the horses they were riding were about done in.

"You know them good, do ya?" asked Ben.

"Yes sir."

"You need the help," said Jennie, "and you are the boss, so we will leave that up to you."

Mason smiled, "Can I bunk them down in Carlos old house?"

"That's a good idea," said Ben, "that will make us a good bunk house."

"I bet they don't know a damn thing 'bout workin' cows," said Ben.

"Nope, but I bet it won't be long till they do, Mason will see to it."

"I sure hope they work out, we shore need the help," said Ben.

"I just hope we find out their names?"

"Virgil and Benny Pitts," said Mason. "They are my mama's brother's boys. We was raised together, till paw moved us to Texas. They don't know much about ranching, but they will learn, if ya'll will give 'um time."

When winter ended and with spring in the air, Mason got spring roundup started and Mason was right. Virgil and Benny learned quick. They were becoming good cowboys. The roundup was going good. All the hard work was paying off.

"How many steers you think we will have this year?" asked Ben.

"At the last count, we got about 1300 head. By the time we get ready to make the trip to Abilene, we should have another 400 head."

"Lewis, I want you to take Virgil and Benny and go to the Nelson. Round up all the you bulls, cut 'um and brand 'um. Try to keep a count."

With all the spring work complete, they started preparations to make the drive. Only this time they would be going to Dodge City.

Jennie didn't go on this trip. Ben was glad. The farmers were breaking ground. Getting their fields ready to plant. With business good at the store, it was an exciting time around the Baker ranch.

Annie announced that she was pregnant, and Lisa said she was in love.

"May I ask who?" Lisa paused then she blurted out, "Jaun." Jennie sort of figured it. They have spent a lot of time together. "Are you sure it's love?"

"Oh, yes, I am very sure."

"Does he feel the same about you?"

"Yes."

Karla laughed, "He does. Believe me. That is all he talks about."

A representative of the Dallas transportation company, Mr. Watkins, came to see Jennie. He wanted to lease a right of way to build a road and a bridge across the creek. "We will run a stage coach line and a freight line from Dallas to Shreveport. I would like to build a way station here with overnight facilities."

She and Rob had to think about it. "The money will be good, and the extra business will help the store," said Jennie.

"That bridge will change everything. It will be a big help to them farmers. Be a lot of traffic through there, not just wagons, but travelers," said Rob. "But I say yes, it will be good for everybody."

They met with Watkins to set the terms for the agreement. "You will buy your beef from the flying J, and no stores or any other businesses built on that property period," said Rob.

"Of course not, all we are interested in is travel."

"You bring us a contract, we'll sign it," said Rob.

"One more thing," said Mr. Watkins, "I want to establish a post office here, but I need a name for this place. What can we call it?"

"Jennieville," said Rob.

"Sounds good to me, and you will have to provide the space in the store, for this post office."

"Damn," said Rob, "what else?"

Mr. Watkins smiled. "Recon, I kinda piled it on quick, but I don't think you will regret it."

"I hope not, I surely do." Jennie said.

"It seems when I opened that store, things started popping," said Jennie.

Annie was washing dishes, Jennie was drying them, Maria was mopping the floor. Maria spoke up, "One thing we have had here was privacy. I don't think that will ever be again."

Business at the store was booming. The road crew, the bridge crew and the men building the way station, all spent money at the store. Rob and Jennie picked up the profits from the store at the end of the week.

"We got a problem here Rob, we got to buy a safe, this is a lot of money."

"And Ben will be home shortly with a lot more," said Rob.

"I am worried about him, I hear all the stories about Indians, rustlers and bandit attacks on the herds heading north."

"It is more dangerous than it was last year," said Rob, "but they will make it."

They did make it, but not without incidents. They got in a shooting scrape with some rustlers. Manny got shot in his hand. It got infected. Ben took him to the first doctor they came to. It was bad. The doctor had to amputate his hand at the wrist. Ben left him there and went on to Abilene. He picked him up on the way back.

Manny was the focus of everybody's attention, especially Maria. Jennie told Ben about the road and the bridge. "When you go to the store, it will amaze you."

"And we getting paid for all that?"

"Yep, and the store is making more money than any of us could have imagined."

"Well, well, sounds like good fortune has fell on this family alright."

After Ben got a couple of days' rest, Rob and Annie met with him and Jennie. Ben put over 27000 dollars on the table. Rob leaned back in his chair. "We are rich."

Jennie didn't serve coffee this time. She sat four glasses and a bottle of whiskey on the table. They talked for hours, making plans. In the end, they all agreed. Then Ben spoke up, "One thing is for sure."

Said Jennie, "we got to build another barn. We need it for the corn." They all agreed.

"One more thing," Ben said, "I would like to do. We made Mason our range boss, and he is doing a good job."

"I would like to put Jaun in charge of the horses and the barns. Somebody needs to keep up with that stuff. I think he will be a big help to Mason. We got horses running wild on this ranch. We need to round them up, and start breeding them proper, and braking to the saddle harness like before, and he can deal directly with them farmers."

Jennie and Rob looked at each other. "You know something," said Rob, "you are right."

"I think that is a good idea, a damn good idea."

"Me too," said Jennie. "I think you should do just that."

"I will," they all laughed. It was the way Ben said it, plus the whiskey was taking effect.

Annie got up from the table. "Rob, I think maybe you orta take me home." That brought on another big laugh.

"I think you are right." It was hard to tell who was holding up who when they walked across the yard.

Jaun was reluctant at first. He felt he wasn't qualified. "I think you could find somebody with more experience to do that job."

"Yeah, I am sure we could, but we want you," said Ben.

Jaun shook his head slowly, "I don't know."

"I do, and you can start right now."

"Start? I don't know where to start."

Ben mounted his horse, "You will figure it out. One more thing, I want you to get Manny to help you and get him off that porch, feelin' sorry for himself."

He watched Ben ride away. He turned to face his horse, "damn." He slapped his hat against his leg. His horse jerked his head up, "One minute I am like you, just go where I am told to go, do what I am told to do. One minute later, I got a load of responsibility. Well, maybe I don't want all that responsibility. He never asks me, he just told me."

Jaun walked back and forth in front of his horse, talking. He stopped. "Manny, boy that will be a tough one. He can be hardheaded."

Manny refused Jaun. "I can't help you, look, I only got one hand."

He went to Ben, "He said no, he thinks he is helpless."

"I have been thinkin' on this, I think maybe I got an idea. Let me work on it some."

Ben told Carlos his idea. Carlos was good with leather. When he was finished, he took it to Ben.

"That's exactly what I want. Carlos, you are good."

"If only Manny will wear it."

"He'll wear it alright," said Ben.

Ben went into Manny's room. Carlos and Maria followed him. He handed Manny the cup. It had a hook on one end. Two straps with a leather ban to wrap around his arm just above his elbow. Manny sat looking at it.

"It ain't gonna put itself on, you gotta help a little," said Ben.

"I gotta put this thing on every morning for the rest of my life?"

"Yep, and you gotta put your damn pants on every morning and your damn boots." He put his face close to Manny's face.

"Put it on," said Ben in a stern but low voice.

Slowly, Manny slipped it on his arm. "I can't tie it."

Maria hurried over and tied it for him. He put his shirt on.

"Come with me," said Ben. He had Manny's horse tied outside. The reins were tied together and hanging over the pommel of the saddle.

"Manny, take that hook and put it around that pommel and get up in the saddle. Now, pick up them reins with that hook and give them twist." Ben took his hat and slapped Manny's horse on the rump. He took off, heading for the creek.

Manny went across the creek at a dead run. He reined in his horse and turned around. He rode back the same way, coming to a sliding halt in front of the house, "Is that what you wanted to see?"

Ben smiled a big smile, he slapped Manny on his leg. "Yep, that's what I wanted to see alright."

Manny grew more comfortable with the hook. He learned how to use it, and as time passed he didn't think about his handicap. They spent days at a time away from the ranch house. The flying J was a big ranch. Jaun and Manny rounded up all the horses they could find. They kept them in a pasture close to the ranch house.

Mason sat on his horse alongside Jaun. They looked out over the herd of horses.

"How many you got?" asked Mason, as he rolled a cigarette.

"About 45 or 50, is my guess."

"That's a good number."

"I got to separate them work horses from the saddle ponies."

"Sounds like we need some fences," said Mason. "We can talk to Ben about that."

"How's the barn coming along?"

"It should be finished in three or four days."

"Mason, I gotta speak with you."

"Go ahead, what is it?"

"It's about me and Lisa."

Mason turned to look at him, "yeah, what about you and Lisa?"

"We want to get married."

Mason cocked his head to one side, "What?" Jaun just looked at him. Mason looked away, then back at Jaun, "She wants to marry you?"

Jennie and Lisa were glad their husbands were not going. Jennie knew from firsthand how hard and dangerous.

"Damn Jaun, this catches me off guard. I didn't know you and her were that serious." He sat there a minute, "Well if marrying you will make her happy, then I am all for it, hell yeah." They shook hands, "But you know we still gotta make it alright with mama?"

It was the biggest wedding ever in that part of the country. Annie had her baby, a girl. They named her Mary Sue Baker.

Jennie and Ben had come to the conclusion, they could not have children, for whatever reason. "Some folks just can't have babies," said Ben.

CHAPTER 20

It was a good year for them. They had more money than any of them ever dreamed of. Ben and Mason stood by the corral talking. Virgil and Benny came riding up.

"You boys look out of breath," said Ben.

"We got a problem," said Virgil.

"What kind of problem?" asked Ben.

"Rustlers."

"Are you sure about that?"

"Yep."

Mason told us to take them longhorns over to 9. "Then take that bull ole lazy boy, over there."

"When we got them there, the longhorns was gone. We found their trail, along with some horse tracks."

"Damn," said Mason.

"We been lucky so far, it had to happen sooner or later."

Ben kept his horse at the house that night. He woke up well before daylight. He eased out the door, trying not to wake Jennie. He threw his saddle on his horse. He saw a light come on in the barn. The light went out. He could see a man leading a horse, come from the barn.

Ben mounted up and followed him. He didn't know for sure who it was, but he had a good idea. Ben rode up alongside Mason. "You planning to catch them rustlers all by yourself was ya?"

Mason didn't turn his head, "Well, something like that."

Section nine was in the far south west corner of the ranch. It would be tomorrow before they got there. It was mostly open pasture, and they knew the lay of the land, so they rode at a fast gallop. They stopped at a stream to let the horses rest and fill up on water. They filled their water bags then walked over and sat down under a tree. They rested for half an hour. Ben stood up, "If you ready, we will make tracks." Mason got to his feet, "I'm ready."

Ben climbed up into the saddle. "I am glad you are here," Ben said.

"Ya, and I am glad you are here."

They both laughed. They crossed the stream, then up the ridge on other side and stopped in a grove of scrub oaks. They tied their horses with a short rope and took off the bridles and loosened the cinch. Ben took his saddle bags and went a few feet away. He started a small fire, then took a small coffee pot from the saddle bags.

"Mason, I didn't bring no extra cup."

"I did, a cowboy has always got a cup with him."

Ben laughed, "That's true. I did bring some biscuits and a few cans of food."

"I brought some biscuits and meat left from supper and a big hunk of ham." They sat eating and drinking their coffee. The sun was sliding down. It was sitting right on the horizon.

"This is some pretty country alright." Said Mason.

"Yes it is."

Ben woke up first. He put some wood on the fire and got it started. Mason rolled over. "I am stiff as aboard. Been a long time since I slept on the ground." He sat up and rolled a cigarette.

"Coffee is ready," said Ben. They rode for two hours without stopping. Ben held up his hand. They slowed to a stop. "Recon, we better give these horses a break." Ben said. They gave them some water, and let them rest. Ben pointed across the landscape.

"See that hill there with the trees on it?"

"Yeah, I see it."

"We will go there and make camp. Yep, I think that will be a good place."

Mason did not know what Ben had in mind, but whatever it was, he was with him. They made camp, then hobbled the horses and let the graze. From where they sat, they could see for over two miles in all directions. Ben took a field glass from his bag. He scanned the landscape.

"Can I asked, what you expect to see?"

"Smoke," Ben stopped. He handed the glass to Mason, and pointed, "See it?"

"Yep, smoke, I be damned, I never would have thought about this. But won't they see our smoke?"

"Probably not, but I hope they do. That'll worry them some. Make 'um think maybe some more rustlers done run in on 'um."

Mason grinned, "You somethin' else."

"I was a Texas ranger longer than I been a rancher. If them assholes stay here, I'll catch 'um, you can bet on that."

"I dealt with rustlers before. My paw hung one. Hung a few myself."

"Glad you are here Mason. You know what we up against with these fellas."

"We going to head for that smoke?"

"Na, they will be gone by the time we get there."

"Good, I don't think them horses are up to it anyway."

"Mason, sometimes it pays to pause and have a good look around, ya know."

After breakfast, they saddled up and headed in the direction of the smoke they had seen yesterday. They found some tracks. Ben was standing on the ground. He looked off to the west, "We'll just follow these tracks."

Most of section nine was fairly good for grazing, and there was water. Ben has never been here. Mason came once about a year ago. They were on the edge of their property. The grass gave way to sand and large boulders, and had a lot of ravines and gullies. There were only a few scrubby trees around. But no water.

They followed the tracks, moving slow, stopping to look around. The last thing Ben wanted was to get ambushed.

"What do you think?" Mason asked.

"We got a hot trail here Mason. I ain't never been lucky enough to find a fresh trail like this. Yeah, we might be lookin' in a bear cave, with a mean mama bear inside."

"But you gone keep goin'?"

Ben smiled, "Yep."

"Well, lead on, Mr. Bear Hunter."

It was getting late, so they made camp. The next day, Ben found what he was looking for. The trail led them into a dead end gully. It was empty. The rustlers were gone.

"They couldn't have stayed here long," Ben said, "no water, no grass." The rustlers built a brush arbor for shade. Mason knelt down and felt of the ashes in the little fire pit, "Cold."

They went back to the entrance. They found tracks leading farther west. Ben squatted down. "Damn. I hate to get this close, and quit." He stood up and swung up in the saddle. "But we got no choice. We almost out of grub and water. There ain't nothing around here to eat or drink, that's for sure."

"They will be back," Mason said. "As soon as they spend their money."

"I think you are right," said Ben. It was shady on that side of the ravine.

"These horses are tired," said Mason.

He dismounted and took the saddle and bridle off his horse. Then gave him some water. They sat in the shade for an hour, then headed back. It was a long ride back to the edge of the flying J property. When they finally got to water, it was almost dark. They made camp for the night, and ate the last of their food. Both men slept late the next morning. They drank the last of the coffee, then broke camp.

It was about noon the next day when they rode into the barn. After taking care of the horses, they went to their houses. Jennie wasn't at home, so Ben walked over to the big house. Maria fixed him a plate of leftovers. Then he went to his house. He stripped off naked and lay across the bed.

He lay there thinking, "How dumb he was to leave home without a pack horse. How stupid," was his last thought before he fell asleep. Ben woke up, he heard Jennie rambling around in the next room. She peaked in the bedroom, "I see you are awake, don't get dressed, I got a hot bath ready for you."

When he walked into the room, Jennie was pouring a pan of hot water into the big wash tub. After he wash his hair and face, he just sat there soaking. Jennie had a plate of eggs and bacon cooked. She knelt down beside the tub and feed him while he told her what him and Mason found out, and how he let them get away.

When he was finished eating, she went into the bedroom. She left the door open. She took off her clothes and sat on the bed.

"Like what you see?" she asked with a grin on her face.

"Oh yeah, what man wouldn't like a body like that?" He walked over and took her face in his hands, "and a beautiful face to go with it."

CHAPTER 21

It was a cold winter. Ben told Mason to build three line shacks, with corrals and sheds for winter hay. "One in sections 3, 6, and 9, and stock them with can goods, I don't plan on getting caught like we did, chasing them rustlers."

Mason hired three ranch hands to help with spring round up, Shorty, Tucker and Ace. All three were in their mid-twenties. They would make him good hands. Honest and hard workers.

Jaun hired a young boy, he was maybe 17 years old at the most. "Just call me John," he said, "don't have no last name." He liked horses, and working with them. He was always up and ready to work before daylight.

With the hint of spring in the air, everybody had a little bounce in their step. Ben and Mason decided to take a tour of the ranch and get an estimate or at least a rough estimate of newborn calves. They were in section 4 west of the ranch house. Mason reined in his horse, "is that gun fire?"

Ben cocked his head, "sounds like it."

"Coming from that directions," said Mason.

"Let's go see who is shooting, and what they are shooting at."
They rode about a mile, Ben held up his hand. "They had to be
around here."

"I'd say so."

They rode slow, looking for signs. Mason rode along the edge
of a gully. "Ben, come look." They both stared down into the gully.
They saw the bodies of dead Indians. "I say 10 or so," said Mason.
Ben rode down into the gully and dismounted. He walked from
body to body, "What was they doing here? I ain't never seen no
kiawas here."

Mason knelt down beside a woman, she had been shot in the
back, "Ben this one is alive."

"Yeah, and she ain't no kiawa neither."

Mason gently turned her on her back. When he did, he saw a
baby. In a weak voice she said, "Don't kill my baby, please."

"No ma'am," said Mason. "We ain't gonna hurt nobody."

"Thank you," her head rolled to one side.

"She's gone." Ben reached down and picked up the baby.

"What now?" asked Mason.

"I recon we will take this here baby home with us."

Jennie sat on the front porch of her house. Ben rode up and
dismounted.

"What you got there?" He walked up on the porch. She looked
at the baby, "Ben, where did you get that child?"

"Here, take it. Come inside, I will tell ya what happened." Ben
told her what they saw while Jennie took care of the baby.

"Ben, it's a girl. She can't be more than 8 or 9 months old."
Jennie wrapped her in the blanket. "Let's go see Annie. She will
have what I need. This child is hungry, and needs a bath."

It was obvious to Ben that Jennie wasn't listening to a word he said. He followed her across the yard.

Mason had told everybody what had happened. Within an hour, the house was full. As they heard the news, they came to the big house and they were all there full of questions.

"We got no answers to them question, in fact, questions are all we have got," said Ben.

"And a little baby kiawa girl," said Maria.

"And a little half breed kiawa girl," repeated Ben. "That baby's mother was a white woman."

Ben got to his feet, "boys, get some shovels, we got some buryin' to do."

Ben rode with Rob in the buckboard. They took a tour around the ranch. Rob liked to get out, away from the house. Some days his knee hurt, he would sit on the porch, with his leg propped up. Today, it was fine.

"Ben, you know Jennie is growing very fond of that baby."

"I do know that."

"Does it bother you?" He didn't answer for a minute. "Raising a Kiawa Indian here in Texas, even if she is half white, will cause problems down the road."

"Maybe the world will be different by the time she gets grown."

"Maybe, but all these folks will be dead before any changes are made."

Jennie sat on the front porch, she was rocking the baby. Ben sat down in the other chair beside her.

"Did you and Rob have a nice day?"

"Oh yeah."

"I think he really enjoys the days he spends with you."

"I do too, I have always liked him."

Mason and Rex rode up to the house. They went to Jennieville for Jennie. They picked up the money from the store. He put the bag on the table.

"Thanks Mason," she said.

"It was a pleasure. Ben, can I talk to you a minute?"

"Sure," he followed Mason out into the yard.

"I just thought you might like to know. When I was at the store, I overheard a conversation about some Kiawas that escaped while they was being moved to the reservation. The army sent some scouts and soldiers to bring them back. Word is the Kiawas put up a fight, and they all got killed."

Ben hung his head, "Well mason, I guess we'll just have to let it ride. Ain't nothin' we gonna say or do to change it."

"That's why I didn't say anything."

"Let's keep it to ourselves, okay?"

Jennie feed the baby and put her to bed. Then she sat down with Ben to eat their supper. "Ben, we need to talk about the baby."

"Well talk."

"I think you know, but I'll say it. I want to keep this child and raise it as our own."

"It may cause us trouble down the road. Are you willing to deal with it?"

"Yes, and I know as well as you, how people feel. It's you that matters to me."

"I will be happy to help you raise her, but I am tired of calling her the baby. Maybe you should give her a name." Jennie got up, she sat in his lap, "I love you." She gave him a long kiss. She leaned back with her arms around his neck, "Martha."

"Martha," he said.

"Yep, Martha Adams."

"Alright, Martha it is."

CHAPTER 22

With spring round in full swing, Mason hired four new hands. "They have made two cattle drives," he told Ben. "I plan to take them with me. Having experienced drovers will help."

"Good, that's good. You should be ready to go shortly," Ben said.

"I figure 10 days, maybe two weeks."

Jaun had the remuda ready. Manny and John would go on the drive. Jaun reluctantly agreed to stay home. "They will do fine," said Mason. "Them boys know horses good as anybody."

A week before they left, Mason hired a cook. He had his own wagons and a helper. "I specialize in cattle drives," he said, "and I am a damn good cook. Gotta keep them drovers happy, bad food will turn um sour," he said. "Just call me Cookie and this here is my helper, Ham Bone, his name is Willis, but call him Ham Bone."

He decided on his trail crew. He chose Virgil and Benny, also Shorty, Tucker and Ace, and the four new hands. Mason left the ranch with over 1300 steers. Ben was kinda disappointed, that he wasn't going with him, so was Rex and Lewis.

The three of them rode up on top of the rise, from here they could see the herd as they stretched out and headed north. "Well, there they go," said Rex.

Jaun come riding up and joined them. He had been with Manny, giving last minute advice how these drives can be.

Ben hired some fence builders. They were to build a series of corrals, so Jaun could keep the work horses separated from the saddle ponies. They were staking off where the fences were to go, when Rex and Lewis rode up.

"Them rustlers are back," said Rex.

"Are you sure?" asked Ben.

"Yes sir."

"They can't be after steers."

"They got brood cows," said Lewis, "some of our prime stock."

Ben dropped the wooden stakes. "Let's go to the house, we need to get fresh horses and supplies."

"I am going with you," said Jaun.

At first, Ben thought no, but he might need the extra gun, "Let's go." Ben was going to take the chance that these were the same rustlers, and they would hold the cattle in the same ravine.

They spent the night at the line shack in section 9. The horses got a good rest and feed.

Ben pushed hard the next day by traveling in a straight line. They saved nearly half a day. Ben crawled up to the edge of the ravine. "Damn, either they were already gone with the cows, or they were never."

He led the way into the mouth of ravine. "They was here all right," said Rex, "these are fresh tracks."

"This time will be different," Ben thought. "We got food and water." They followed the trail till dark, then made camp.

"We orta catch up with them tomorrow," said Lewis. Ben walked over and saddled his horse.

"Where you goin'?" asked Jaun.

"Them fellas can't be too far ahead of us. I will be back. Don't shoot me."

It was still light enough for Ben to follow the trail, but dark was closing in fast. He traveled slow, picking his way cautiously. He stopped often to listen. He dismounted and walked, he felt the ground. He could feel the tracks left by the cows. He decided to head back, he froze. He saw a flicker of light. He walked a little closer. There, now he could see it better. A campfire, maybe 100 yards, "Well, well, so I found ya."

He stood thinking, then he tied his horse, and took his spare pistol from the saddle bag. Ben knew he was taking a big chance, but he had the element of surprise. He slipped through the trees till he was close enough to see the men sleeping around the fire. He counted three. He looked out at the herd bedded down about 20 yards away.

He spotted one man on horseback. Ben eased closer to him, the rider was slumped over. "He is asleep," he thought. Ever so cautious, he made his way to within a few feet, he took his knife and threw it. The knife stuck in his back. He straightened up, then fell from the saddle.

Ben rushed over to him. The man was dead. He caught the man's horse and took hold of the reins. He looked at the cows. They were not moving, so everything was okay. He tied the horse, then made his way back to the campfire.

"My luck is holding out so far." Ben took both pistols from his holsters, then a deep breath, he exhaled, "Well, here goes nothin'."

He walked to the edge of the light and fired a shot into the air. The men were startled and disoriented. Which is exactly what Ben expected.

"Reach for the sky boys." They all froze. "That's it, just stay where you are. Don't, nobody move." They didn't speak, they just stood there looking at Ben and the two pistols pointed at them. "Well boys, take your feet and kick them guns over this way. Then lay down on your bellies with your hands behind your backs."

He tied their hands, then he tied them to a tree. "If you thinkin' your buddy out there will come in here and shoot me, forget it, he's dead." Finally, one man asked, "Who are you?"

"The man that owns them cows."

"You plannin' to hang us are ya?"

"Yep."

"You done scared our horses off, and scattered them cows. Seems like you gone have a lot work to do."

"You just relax, and let me worry 'bout all that."

When daylight came, he fired three shots into the air. He hoped in the early morning calm, one of his men would hear the shots. They came riding in. Rex sat on his horse, "What the hell is going on here?"

Jaun dismounted, "Looks like the boss done hog tied him some rustlers to me."

"You got here quick enough," said Ben.

"We got worried about you," said Rex. "We was over half way here when we heard them shots."

With the job of hanging the rustlers behind them, they rounded up as many cows as they could find and headed home.

"I do hope I don't ever have to hang nobody else," said Jaun.

"You don't ever get used to."

Mason returned to the ranch with another big payday. He filled them in on what happened, from the time he left till he got back. Cookie and Ham bone stayed in Dodge City, along with the four drovers. "They said if we made another drive next year, they would be here. They are good help. I told them to be here."

"Good," said Ben.

"One of the drovers, called Ed, got shot. I sent him to Snellville with Ham bone. You know the place we get supplies? Well, he went to the saloon, got in a gunfight. He killed one man and wounded another. He is a tough one. His wounds were not bad. He caught up with us a few days later."

Jaun was glad to hear that Manny and John did a good job. He told Ben he was proud of Manny, "He owes it all to you."

"Not just me, you and Carlos helped."

They all had news to tell. They all ate at the big house, then sat and talked way into the night.

Rob's leg got worse. It was constant pain. Jennie and Annie spent a lot of time every day on the porch with him. They let the kids play. Rob had a banister built to keep the girls from falling off the porch.

Noah Martin played in the yard. Sometimes, he went with Ben or Mason. They took a lot of time with him. Noah liked being away from the house. Jennie and Annie were inside the house. Annie watched Rob on the front porch. He was asleep in his rocking chair.

"Jennie, I just don't know what to do. He is in such pain. The only sleep he gets is when he drinks enough of that whiskey, it knocks him out. I think he is addicted to that painkiller too. I know he can't stand it much longer."

A few days later, Rob got a letter. It was from a doctor in Dallas. That night, he announced that he was going to take the stage to Dallas. "I wrote to Doctor Benjamin. He has agreed to see me as soon I get there. I'll be leaving tomorrow."

"I am going with you," said Annie.

"Oh no, I will be going alone." She protested.

"No, Annie, I mean it."

She started crying and ran into her bedroom. Jennie followed her.

"That ain't fair, Rob," Ben voiced his disapproval also.

"Come with me, Ben." Rob limped outside on the porch. "Ben, I am not sure what will happen when I get there. He may cut my leg off. I do know I have got to do something. If the pain doesn't stop, I will put a bullet in my brain. Either way, I don't want her there."

The family watched the stagecoach leave Jennieville. Annie cried all the way home. She sat on the porch every day, just rocking and waiting.

The days turned into weeks, with no word. Finally, Jaun brought two letter to Annie. One was from Rob. The other was from Doctor Benjamin. She opened Rob's letter first. He told her how much he loved her and the kids.

"It was almost like a goodbye letter," she said to Jennie. When she read the doctor's letter, she fainted. Jennie and Maria got her up and took her to her bed.

Jennie read the letter. She put her hand over her mouth and sat down on the bed. She looked at Maria, "He is dead Maria, my brother is dead."

Ben read the letter to everybody. They were all gathered outside in the front yard. "He died of complications, from the amputation. The doctor cut his leg off, then it got infected. The

doctor is sending his body back at Rob's request. Rob paid for everything, before he died."

Annie would not get up from her bed. She just lay there with her face pressed into her pillow. "Just leave her there," Maria said. "She will be fine."

Ben sent the hands to dig a grave. "We want to be ready when the body gets here."

The funeral was short. They were all there by the little graveyard by the creek. Jennie walked to the wagon where Ben was waiting. "They are all gone, Ben. My whole family. Look! They are all right there in the ground." She put her face in his chest and cried.

When Annie got back to the house, she went straight to her room. It will take her some time to get over Rob's death.

<h1 style="text-align:center">CHAPTER 23</h1>

Jaun and Lisa had a boy. Now, Carlos and Maria were happy grandparents. They named him Robert Santos.

Jennie's days were filled with young Martha. It was a labor of love. Being there tending to, gave her time to think. Every day when Ben came home, after they ate supper and put Martha to bed she would tell him her ideas.

Ben would sit there and listen. Partly amused and partly interested. She talked none stop with so much enthusiasm. Something she never did before. Jennie heard a knock at the door. It was Maria. "Come in, have a seat." Maria sat at the table.

"Can I get you something to drink, some coffee maybe?"

"No thanks." Jennie sat down across the table.

"Is something on your mind?"

"Yes, it's Annie. She just mopes around. I can't get her interested in her children's housework, nothing. I know she misses Rob."

Jennie took Maria's hand. "You want me to talk to her?"

"I think you should."

"Alright, tomorrow. I will see what I can do."

The next morning after Ben left, Jennie took Martha, and went to see Annie. Annie sat at the kitchen table drinking coffee. Jennie sat down. Maria brought her a cup of coffee, then left them alone. They made small talk for a few minutes.

"Jennie, I can't get it off my mind. All I can think about is he died all alone." She looked up, with tears in her eyes. "Why?"

Jennie didn't answer. She sat there in silence. Annie stared into the cup.

"Why didn't he let me go with him?" Still Jennie said nothing.

Annie looked up. "Why Jennie? Just tell me why." After a few seconds of silence, Jennie spoke.

"I can't answer that question. Nobody can. We will never know why." Jennie put Martha on the floor. She was learning to crawl.

"The thing is, I think you are mad."

"Mad, about what?"

"He didn't let you go. You are mad at him for that." Annie looked at Jennie with a puzzled look.

"That's right. You are mad at Rob for not letting you go with him. I can hear the anger in your voice." Annie didn't say anything, she just looked at Jennie.

Jennie stood up. She walked over and picked Martha up and placed on her hip. Then walked out. They didn't speak.

A few days later Lisa came and took Martha back to her house.

Jennie sat on the porch. She waved by to them. "You be a good little girl. Lisa, if she gets cracky, you bring her on home."

"I will, but don't worry she will be fine."

Annie watched out her window. When Lisa left, she walked over and joined Jennie on the porch.

"Mind if I join you?"

"Of course not, have a seat." They talked for a few minutes, then Annie grew quit. Jennie sat looking out across the yard.

"Jennie, I think maybe you are right. I think I am angry, but I don't know what to do about it."

"I was angry too, I am still angry. My feelings were hurt. I have always been close to Rob. I can't answer all the question we have, but he didn't leave here thinking he would die. I know he loved you very much. You were everything to him. He loved his kids. He thought he was doing right by you. I do believe that. You know Rob, what you are thinking never crossed his mind. You have to start today and make him proud of those two kids. Live, grow, don't wilt away." Annie listened as Jennie talked. She was right. She could see now that she was accusing him of things he didn't intend or even think about doing.

"I have let my imagination run wild, Jennie." She stood up and walked off the porch. She stopped at the bottom of the steps. "Thanks Jennie."

Noah Martin was old enough now to help around the ranch. He went with Mason every chance he got. He liked working with cows. He liked ranch work. Annie was having trouble getting him to do his chores around the house.

She told Mason. "I want him to do his job around here first, then he can tag along after you."

"Alright I will tell him."

"You do that."

Sarah was turning into a good cook and housekeeper. She was a big help to Maria. They cooked meals for the ranch hands.

Jennie and Annie had taught all the children to read, write spelling, and to add and subtract. Sarah was a bright girl. Math came easy for her. She sat with Jennie sometimes when she did the books. Sarah asked questions. Jennie tried to tell her what she was doing, and why. "Someday, she will take over this job."

Jennie and Ben sat on the porch. "Jennie, I think this ranch will be in good hands when we get too old to run it."

"Yes it will. I am very proud of the people we have working here. I am proud of our family. They are all hard workers, honest and just good people."

Martha walked up to Jennie. She picked her up and put her in her lap. "And I am so proud of you too, little girl."

THE END